The Thornless Rose

Fire Blush

Samantha Fidler-Newby

To Mom and Tom

Thank you for pushing and supporting me all this time.

We did it!

Chapter 1

A pair of sapphire eyes appeared, unnoticed, in the crack of the oak doors as Lord Bion and his brother, Marcus, quietly argued about what lay on the table by the fireplace. Firelight danced on the walls as Viviana watched the men's faces and listened to the argument escalate. She listened to their voices, but she could not pull her eyes away from the object on the table. The blood-soaked sheet rose and fell, as if alive. The sound of a fist hitting the wooden table snapped her attention back to the two men in the room.

"You must call for her and you know it," the shorter of the two men growled. She gasped as she realized blood caked them from their heads to their boots.

"I know he needs her, but I fear what she must face. He knows so much. If he tells her anything, all will be for naught…all he has sacrificed." Viviana's father sighed and sat in his chair. His body shuddered under the weight of his decision. "I will call on her if he becomes worse in the next hour. I do not want to bring her here unless I absolutely have to." He looked towards the door. She quickly pressed against the frame and waited for the men to start talking again, giving her the chance to escape down the hall.

Swiftly, she moved down the corridor and used a hidden passageway leading to another empty hall. In moments, her cloaked figure found a small staircase lit by the moonlight streaming through stained glass windows. A single door at the top of the stairs opened to a small bedroom, furnished with beautiful oak dressers and a four-post bed. The opened curtains fluttered when the door closed, and a small noise escaped Viviana's mouth. She quickly removed the cloak and let her dark, amber hair cascade down her back. After jumping into bed, Viviana waited for sleep to come, but her mind was filled with questions. *What was that on the table? Whom must she save?* Flipping open the leather-bound book where she kept all her important thoughts and feelings, Viviana wrote fervently until a knock on her door made her jump. She quickly hid the journal.

"Viviana, may I come in?" a deep, husky voice asked from the other side of the door.

"Of course, Father," her honey-sweet voice answered. As she watched him come in, she hoped he did not notice her cloak was out of place. She glanced at her healer's bag lying by the door, ready with all her supplies.

Her father slowly entered with a lantern that lit the entire room, but he would not look at her. He looked like a man on the verge of collapsing, and it startled her.

"What is wrong? Why are you crying?" She sat up in bed as he sat by her feet. He motioned for her to give him a hug.

"My little girl…my only child…I have a heavy boon to ask of you," he said as he held her close.

"What happened? Is someone injured?" The look on his face twisted her stomach in knots. She knew *that* look.

"Why do you think someone is hurt?" he asked, puzzled by her question.

"You are crying, and you do not cry, Father. Did someone die?"

"No, but…he is close to it." He tried to clear away the tears from his face.

She paused for a moment and understood what he was asking from her. The toll on her body from healing a person on death's door was unknown. There was no way of telling if she could even manage it. Whomever she was to save, he must be important.

Her eyes met his and she gave him a weary smile. "I will do whatever I can. Who is it?"

"Your cousin, Anthony. I need, I mean he, needs your healing touch. He is barely hanging on, and it would kill your aunt and uncle if they lost him. Your Aunt Mathilda has done all she can for him, but he needs more. I know what this might do to you…" he trailed off as he looked into her eyes. She placed her hand on his.

"I know how this affects you, Vi," he continued. "The last time you healed someone, you were unconscious for almost a day. He is badly beaten and bruised, but I do not want to put you in danger again."

Viviana jumped from the bed and was met with a strong bear hug from her father.

"We should hurry," she said, inhaling the scent of blood and dirt on her father's clothes. She went to the door to gather her healer's bag and shoes.

"Would you put some clothes on, please?"

"Oh," she picked up her cloak from the bed and put it on.

He sighed and guided her to the door. "I will have Rox get you something decent when the sun rises."

Her father was right; no one knew what would happen to her if she used her gift on someone on the verge of death. Her last patient had only broken her arm. The pain she felt afterward lingered for several days, but no one knew about that. They worried enough about her and her abilities as it was.

As they continued down the hall, she stayed close to her father and tried to steady her breathing. She could not let her nerves get the best of her at this moment. This mysterious cousin needed to be rescued. Playing back her childhood memories, Viviana did not recall Anthony, though she was very close to his sister, Adilynn.

She snapped out of her thoughts when the stench of blood and Aunt Mathilda's wound paste assaulted her nose.

"What happened?" she whispered to her father.

"We do not know for sure," he whispered back to her. "We will have to wait until…"

He believed so much in her gift that it made her stomach lurch. What if she could not bring him back? The thought made her cringe, especially when she saw her aunt and uncle. Uncle Marcus was leaning against the wall in the corner, while her aunt mixed the herbs and oil together. Viviana recognized the mixture by the scent. It was the strongest medicine her aunt knew for pain.

The sight of her cousin's body on the table made her wonder if it was too late. She banished that thought from her mind; this was her relative, the son of her dearest aunt and uncle. They looked up from the table, and their eyes filled with hope. Mathilda moved from her son to her husband and clung to him as she watched Viviana approach the body.

Viviana set her bag down and took her father's lantern, placing it close to her cousin to see the full extent of the injuries. When she removed the cover, she gasped. The wounds were deep, some of them to the bone. She had to move quickly.

What could cause such severe wounds? she asked herself.

"We believe that it was some type of beast," her father whispered to her as if reading her mind. "The wounds are too severe to be caused by human hands."

Aunt Mathilda assisted Viviana by getting a vial from her bag and helping pour half of the emerald-colored liquid down Anthony's throat. Her aunt then stepped away and sat down on a chair. She could do no more for her son.

I must do something different, she thought as she opened a new vial with honey wine in it. Viviana then pricked her finger and let five drops of blood fall into the small bottle. Swirling the contents for a moment, she braced herself for what might happen next.

"What in Heaven's name are you doing with that?" Her uncle sounded shocked by what she had just done.

"The true source of my healing touch is in my blood. I will explain later," Viviana said as she focused on her patient. She asked her aunt to help unwrap Anthony's wounds. The slashed flesh made her gag. She remembered the way she studied patients in the healing house. *Focus on healing the damage.* His muscles and bones were separated in places, and blood was everywhere. She was not sure if the dose was going to be enough since the skin was not patching itself back together. She poured more of her elixir straight onto the wounds, into him. With her aunt's help, she emptied the last of it down his throat. His neck was so badly bruised and beaten that she did not know if he had even swallowed it.

Moments passed and still his breathing was shallow and ragged. Her blood was not working like before, and she panicked. Viviana called forth all her strength and placed her hands on his chest. As she willed his body to mend, she screamed in pain.

"Stop!" her father yelled. She shook her head and kept her hands steady.

"I will heal him," she said and gasped as she saw all the purple bruises and slash marks slowly disappear from her cousin's face. The pain rushed from her fingers up her arms. She needed to let go, but he still needed more. The open wounds were slowly closing before their eyes, and his breathing steadied.

"Let go, Vi," Aunt Mathilda said, taking Viviana's hands off Anthony.

Viviana howled in agony and fell to the ground. Her body convulsed as the room began to spin. Tears flowed from her eyes as the pain ripped through her body. She felt her heartbeat slow, and she could not breathe. Her father's voice calling her name was the last thing she heard as darkness beckoned her into its cold embrace.

Chapter 2

"We knew there would be a price to pay for this, Bion. I am as much to blame as you. Mathilda?" Marcus looked at his wife as she let the tears flow from her eyes.

"Here," Mathilda motioned for Bion to hand over Viviana. Once in her arms, she started to chant and rub her hand over Viviana's face. She felt her becoming cold and stiff. Her tears intensified as she summoned every ounce of essence and placed her hand on Viviana's heart. The color returned to Viviana's face, and she was breathing again. Lord Bion and Marcus breathed a sigh of relief.

"Bion, take her to the healing house." She handed Viviana over. "I fear she gave too much of her essence this time."

"I knew she was powerful, but I had no idea how much our little girl had grown," Marcus said, helping his wife from the floor to the chair by Anthony's side.

"Since she was a child, I knew something was special about her, and she just showed us how special," Mathilda said to her husband as they watched their son's body continue to heal.

The embers burned in the fireplace and sunlight cascaded through the stained-glass windows of the healing house. Four beds lined the walls with medicine cabinets by each one. Fresh herbs and flowers filled the air with their fragrance. Viviana stirred. The sun glistened on her sweaty skin. Her wet hair sat jumbled on top of her head. She moaned, trying to go back to sleep, but her sore body would not let her. Raising her head slightly, she scanned the room and paused. The smell of lavender and roses filled her nose as she noticed the light streaming in from all the windows around her. Then her eyes caught sight of the doorway between the manor and the healing house. It was ajar. *Where is everyone?*

She tried to sit up, but the room started to spin, and her stomach lurched. The pain from last night resonated through her limbs as she tried to move. *Anthony.* His wounded body flashed before her eyes, and she tried desperately to get up from bed.

"Child, what are you doing? Get back in that bed now!" her father scolded her as he rushed into the room.

"Anthony…" she said as she held one side of her head.

"Do not worry about Anthony. He is still recovering, but he is no longer on death's door, thanks to you." He grinned from ear to ear. The pride in his eyes made her happy.

She nodded, which she immediately regretted. Her head still ached. She closed her eyes. Feeling his arms around her, she felt his body shudder as he cried.

"What's wrong, father?" she whispered.

"Your heart stopped beating and you were not breathing. I...thought I killed you..." he said, holding her tighter. She placed her hand on his heart as he gathered himself. "Mathilda tried desperately to revive you, but nothing she did was working. You became cold in her arms." His tears dripped onto Viviana's face as she sat shocked.

I died? But I am here, she thought to herself as Lord Bion dried his face with his sleeve.

"Yet, by some miracle, you came back to me. I knew you were powerful, but I had no idea just how powerful, Viviana," he said, gingerly placing her back in bed, "but now I need you to take your time and rebuild your strength. Do not push yourself."

"Yes, Father." She lay back down, and he kissed her forehead. He closed the door to the healing house and left her alone. Sleep evaded her, so she just stared at the ceiling.

"I can't just lie here," she said aloud. Sitting up, she looked around again. Her stomach hurt. With an intense growl, it reminded her of a primal need. She tested her legs and felt no pain, so she decided to stand again.

"Vi, your father told you to rest," Aunt Mathilda said as she brought in a tray of food. She placed it in front of Viviana, who munched as Mathilda brought in a change of clothes and fresh, hot water for a bath from the healing house spring.

"You are a jewel," Viviana said between bites. "I need to wash this tangled mess on my head." She put her hands to her hair and made a face. As she finished her last morsel of food, she moved slowly to the bathroom. She let Mathilda pour the hot water into the cast iron claw-foot washtub. The steam and heat made Viviana smile.

"How are you feeling, child?" Mathilda checked her over as Viviana tried to get into the bath.

"Not hungry, thanks to you. I'm still sore, but much better than last night." She smiled. It soon faded as she tried to find the right words to ask about Anthony.

"You mean three nights ago," Mathilda said. Viviana's sapphire eyes widened. "Just relax and let me talk. I am astonished you are alive after pouring so much of yourself into healing…Your abilities have grown so much in just these past few years. I had no idea about your blood." Her aunt placed her hand on Viviana's face and looked into her eyes.

"I didn't either until last year. I had cut myself in the kitchen and I bandaged it up before I left to pick wild onion root for you. While in the forest, I found a doe with a large wound in her side. I was going to end her life, but when I touched her, she started to heal. That is when I noticed that my bandage had fallen off, and my blood dripped on her wound. I sat with her and in just an hour or so, the wound was gone, and she ran off into the woods. Remember when Bones was kicked by the horse in the barn? I gave him an elixir, like with Anthony, and placed my hands on him. He healed so quickly, and that was the first time I became ill."

"Last fall?" Mathilda asked, and Viviana nodded. "You never told me." Her aunt sounded hurt.

"I was afraid of what you might say. I feel enough like an oddity with my two abilities. I am not normal, which I accept, but I cannot let people know how unusual I am." She sighed as she motioned for a robe from her aunt.

10

"I have already told the others we must not speak of this." Mathilda kissed her gently on the forehead. "Anthony will know only that you helped aid his recovery. No more, no less. I will do everything to protect you. Your gifts are here for a reason, Viviana, but your secret is safe with us." She moved to the door and motioned for someone to enter. "I will have Coryn aid you further. I have to get back to the kitchen."

"Thank you, Auntie. Let father know how I am doing, and I will make my way to the Dining Hall later. I need to get up and move again. I feel stronger already." She smiled and waved goodbye to her aunt. Viviana sat in a chair by the tub and motioned to her maid to help her with her hair.

"Here is your mirror, Lady Vi," Coryn said.

Viviana felt her maid gently massaging her scalp as she ran a soft brush through her dark amber hair. She could see in the reflection Coryn's cheeks redden on her porcelain face as her silver-colored eyes focused on perfecting the bun on top of Viviana's head. Viviana looked at herself and sighed. Her chubby cheeks made her look much younger than twenty, but her high cheekbones and full lips made up for it.

"My clothes, please." She handed the mirror back to Coryn. As Viviana changed her clothes, she felt a little lightheaded. Her stomach made her realize she was still hungry. She tried to dismiss her maid, but Coryn insisted on finishing Viviana's hair.

"It is fine, Coryn. Please stop fussing," she said as she walked away. Coryn tried her best to keep up with her as she moved swiftly to the Great Dining Hall. The chime of the oak clock in the hall made Viviana stop abruptly, causing her maid to bump into her. The Manor seemed to

11

be less active than normal, as she did not run into any of the guards nor any of the servants.

"Lady Vi, please…I thought you weren't feeling well. Your father will be mad at me if you—" her maid was cut off by the wave of Viviana's hand.

"Please, do not worry, Coryn. I am feeling great, but I'm starving. You can go back to your duties." Her stomach reminded Viviana of her goal and she headed into the kitchen, leaving Coryn behind.

While passing the smaller dining room, she froze. Viviana saw her cousin munching away at a full plate of eggs, sausage, bread, and fruit. He downed a jug of cold milk and she saw some spill a little from the corners of his mouth. His lips parted in a huge grin as he enjoyed his mother's cooking. She was elated at the sight of him sitting there, alive and enjoying himself fully. His carefree smile paired with his well-built body and eyes that had seen the world made her blush. *This is my cousin? He's handsome…so handsome.* She dismissed such foolish ideas as she continued to the kitchen.

"Viviana, you look beautiful as ever." Her aunt wrapped her in a tight hug.

"I…I cannot breathe," she finally managed to get out.

Her aunt let her go but wouldn't stop looking at her. Viviana had saved Anthony from the clutches of the grim beyond. If Viviana knew her aunt, Mathilda would never let her forget it.

"I am sorry, my little one. I am just so happy to see my son—my Andy—alive and looking so vibrant." She took some bread from the oven and handed a plate to Viviana. "You must still be hungry. Here, take whatever you need. Stuff yourself; I want to see you fill out a little more." She grinned as Viviana cringed.

"I am hungry, but please do not try to make me plump. I am going to check on Anthony and see how he is doing. I saw him eating and his color is great. How are the scars?"

"What scars? His body is free of them, at least the ones that would have come from…" She could not talk about the incident yet. Her aunt was still reeling from what happened and looked like she needed some sleep.

"Do you need help? Tell the servants to take care of the cleanup and you go back to bed," Viviana said, trying to guide Mathilda out of the kitchen. Her aunt's skin was pale, and she looked weak.

"Thank you. I might just do that in a little while. There is too much to do for the big dinner," she said as she maneuvered around Viviana to go back to cooking. Nothing could convince her to stop, so Viviana left the kitchen and headed to the dining room.

She turned her attention to her cousin, eating his fill at the table. His sister, Adilynn, was now sitting with him and they were laughing about something. To the untrained eye, they looked like twins. They were tall, lean and had long, wheat colored hair. Both had high cheekbones and sharp noses. The only difference, besides being male and female, were the color of their eyes. Adilynn had eyes as blue as the sky, and Anthony's were the color of the wild, green grass that grew in the fields. They smiled when they saw Viviana.

"Bring that frail body over here. I swear if you don't start eating more, you will never find a man," Adilynn said, taking her plate and giving her a warm but rough hug.

"Well, maybe if you would not take my plate away, I could eat. And besides, who needs a man? I can run this place by myself when father needs me to take over. Either

13

that, or I let Auntie have it and I will go to school. I would be the first woman to graduate from the University." Viviana stroked an imaginary beard and scrunched her face like she was deep in thought, like their old literature professor used to do.

Anthony choked and had milk squirting out of his nose. The girls laughed at his response to Viviana, and he joined in once he could breathe. The ringing of the morning bell was drowned out by the laughter. She handed him a napkin.

"Thanks," he said while wiping his face. "And thank you for what you did for me." He was about as red as the apple sitting on his plate. Viviana did not want to embarrass him any further and changed the subject to the new fashions she saw in the market the other day. She started to discuss a beautiful dress with Adilynn, taking bites of her food throughout the conversation.

Viviana was not skinny, but she was not as plump as most women in her station. She was the daughter of a lord, after all, and was supposed to live a comfortable life, get fat, and marry rich. She was not that kind of girl. Her activities included horseback riding, picking wildflowers, and working around the Manor. The only thing that she even enjoyed about the "comfy life" was being educated like a man and learning to play musical instruments. She also liked learning different types of dance, none her father would approve of.

"Anthony, are you home for good?" Adilynn asked.

"I am not sure what the next step is," Anthony said. "I just had valuable information for Uncle Bion. I don't know who followed me, but I am sure the king will know soon enough."

"The king will know *what* soon enough?" Viviana asked.

"That I am no longer on his side. I am not a loyal knight…" Adilynn kicked him under the table.

The words sent Viviana's head spinning. Anthony was a knight, one of those villainous and cowardly pets of the King of Dragoonus. Just the mere mention of them made her skin grow hot. The flames of the fireplace intensified for a moment as she ran from the room. She flew down the dining hall and didn't stop until she was in her bedroom. Slamming the door behind her, she went to the farthest corner and sat on the floor, panting as she tried to calm her heartbeat. Viviana's mind screamed.

The memories came back, and her blood began to boil. A sizzling sound came from the stones under her hands. She rushed over to the water basin by her vanity and submerged them. The steam calmed her mind, but not her heart. Hot, salty tears poured down her face as she stared at the drawing she made of her mother. *Mother, what do I do? Why is HE a knight? Why did no one tell me?* She curled up in her bed and let the pain flow over her. The body-shaking sobs did not stop until she was so exhausted, she fell into a deep sleep.

Chapter 3

The morning hours passed, and the sun hung low in the afternoon sky. Viviana's whole body ached, and her eyes stung. She slowly pulled herself from her bed, remembering why she secluded herself in her room.

This stranger she was supposed to call cousin was a guard for the king. Her anger flared, but then she remembered his face and those eyes. She saw warmth and kindness in them. *Maybe he isn't a monster, like the others.*

There had to be some reason for her family to keep something so vital from her. She had to believe they loved her; they were her blood, her kin. She needed to talk to her father and find out the truth. A knock at the door made her jump.

"I am so sorry Vi. I should have told you or reminded him of what happened. He would have never mentioned it. I am such a monster," Adilynn said as she rushed in to embrace her cousin. Her eyes were puffy and red. Viviana shook her head and pulled herself from her sweet cousin's arms.

"It was not your fault. He is your brother, and you are wrapped up with him being home and the wedding..." Viviana trailed off, looking over Adilynn's shoulder. Adilynn turned to see what she was looking at. Lord Bion stood in the doorway with Anthony by his side. Viviana could see a mixture of pity and frustration in Anthony's eyes. Her father's face wore the guilt he felt for knowing what she had gone through and the pain it caused her to find out about her cousin's profession. She felt hurt by these two men, for very different reasons, but had no idea how to tell them.

Anthony looked like he wanted to say something, but the words refused to come out. He stared at her, with eyes that begged for her forgiveness. Viviana tried to put on a brave face for her family, but the tears started, and she could not stop. Viviana wanted to be angry, but her father's mighty arms pulled her to his chest, and he whispered repetitively "I'm so sorry." Knowing her father, he was beside himself for making her heal Anthony and not telling her exactly who he was. The tears subsided, but the pain still lingered. She wanted answers.

"I still love you, but I don't like you right now," she whispered, and he hugged her tighter. She saw her cousins holding hands as tears rolled down their faces. Even though they hurt her, she still loved them dearly. The pain was still ever present, but at least Anthony's gentle eyes and warm smile kept her anger at bay, for the moment.

"Let us have a family meeting in the dining hall. Please ask your father and mother to join us," Lord Bion said to Anthony and Adilynn. They nodded and left. "Vi, if you are willing to hear us out, please come with me." He let go of her and moved towards the door.

17

"I will come in a moment and hear what everyone has to say, but I cannot promise I will forgive you. Not yet, anyway," she said. He nodded and bowed deeply. Her father left her alone in her room and she prepared for the meeting.

When she arrived in the dining room, her uncle was standing by her father, while Mathilda and her cousins sat discussing the upcoming nuptials and the guest list. Everyone stopped when they saw her. She took a seat by her father and took a sip from her water cup. Marcus moved to his seat, and they all waited for him to speak. The subject matter for today made everyone uncomfortable.

"First, I would like to say I'm sorry to everyone. I should not have kept Anthony's arrival a secret, but I was unaware he would be here for more than a day or two. His role as a spy for me is critical for the success of our rebellion, and I did not want to put anyone else in danger. Secondly, I am sorry to you, Vi," he said, looking into her sapphire eyes. "I was a fool to keep your cousin's occupation a secret from you. I had no reason to bring you into this matter until he was gravely injured. At that point, I should have told you." He looked away from her as her lip began to quiver. *I must stay calm. I must stay in control.* She reached for her cup but missed and it fell to the floor.

"I'm so clumsy," she said as her cup rolled to the end of the table by Anthony's feet. He picked it up and handed it back to her. She slowly reached out to take it, but their fingers touched for a moment, and she pulled back as if in pain.

"I'm sorry," he said, trying to hand her the cup.

Her heart started to beat faster as she caught a glimpse of the King's Elite Guard Force mark on

18

Anthony's arm, the mark that symbolized the highest ranking for a knight.

"No, I'm fine. Excuse me for a moment," she mumbled as she made her way to the kitchen.

Vivian struggled to catch her breath. Those men were supposed to be the protectors of the weak and uphold the laws. They were once regarded for their valor and heroics on the battlefield, but then a few years ago they started to act more like mercenaries and thieves. Anthony belonged to a group now known for their brutality, the same men who attacked her last year. She was not the only person who had suffered from their hot tempers and sinister motives. The disgust for their kind was more and more common in town, and no matter how much she loved her family, this Anthony was a stranger to her. He was not someone whom she would easily trust herself around. She was in no mood to be around her family any longer, so she made a basket of food and left the kitchen through an unmarked passageway.

She headed out to the barn and hid up in the hayloft where she made her childhood fort so many years ago. When it became hard for her to control her emotions, this is where she came to calm down. Still, her hands trembled, and her mind struggled to concentrate on other thoughts. She watched the sky, perfectly framed by the open window, and enjoyed finding images in the clouds that sauntered by. It started to work its magic. Viviana felt all the muscles in her body relax and she breathed a sigh of relief but knew she would not be able to hide forever.

They would come looking for her soon, but she just didn't feel safe around people at that moment. Her mind focused on the cool summer breeze floating through the air, stirring the birds close to her fort. Their singing made her smile. Gradually, she started to relax and let her thoughts wander.

The memory of the King's Mark came back like a sharp stab in the stomach, and her anger flared again. She always seemed to start trouble when she was angry or upset. When she was only five, she accidentally hurt her father. She didn't know quite how, but when she screamed about getting a doll, he doubled over in pain. She never threw another fit again. The pain in his eyes was too much for her to bear.

Then when she was twelve, her teacher made a rude comment about her capacity to learn from him. He ended up in the healing house with burn marks on his hands from a nearby candle. Her memory was foggy about that day, but she still felt anger for that man. Her mother caught her throwing her book in the fire the next day and scolded her. She made Viviana promise that she would continue her studies and not let the thoughts of foolish people keep her from learning.

To help her with this promise, her mother found her the greatest teacher, Homer. He provided her with an immense amount of knowledge. The most valuable lesson he taught her was a secret Calestius technique of calming emotions and clearing the mind. This always worked for her, until today. The knights still haunted her dreams, and the pain from her healing Anthony was just too fresh for her technique to work. She feared what she might do to her cousin if she couldn't keep calm. He was kin, but that alone may not stop her anger. That alone may not keep her from killing him.

The memory of that horrible night started to play back in her head. She was celebrating her birthday and decided to go out with Adilynn to the best inn in town. The townsfolk knew them well and had great fun celebrating with them. A troupe of actors and dancers brought to town for her joined them at the inn. Viviana danced until her feet were sore. She sat down, looking for Adilynn, but couldn't find her cousin. Feeling uneasy, Viviana made her way outside. She heard her cousin and some unfamiliar voices.

"Please, just leave me alone. I just want to find my friend." Drunken men circled around Adilynn like a pack of wolves.

"Hey Adilynn, there you are. Let's get back in. The troupe wants to escort us back to the Manor," Viviana said, sliding her arm around her cousin and pulling her from the circle.

Viviana could see these men were up to no good. As they headed for the door, one of the men grabbed Viviana's arm.

"Run," Viviana shouted to Adilynn. She ran to the door and disappeared.

"Now since you took our entertainment away, you will have to do," his drunken voice made her skin crawl. She could tell by their clothes they were guards from the capital.

"I am sorry, but my father, Lord Bion, will be missing me, and I should get home." She tried to sidestep one of the guards, but he grabbed her arm again and pulled her back into the circle. His breath stunk of tobacco and cheap wine. As she stood there, one of the men showed her the King's Mark on his arm. They were knights for the king, and it made her pulse quicken with anger.

"Dance for us, whore," one spat at her while slashing at her dress with a small dagger. She screamed and they tried to quiet her with their hands. Her vision blurred and she blacked out. She woke in her bed, exhausted but with a sense of satisfaction. Why, she had no clue. It wasn't until days later that she found out three of the King's guards were dead. One stabbed, the other two badly burned. That was when the nightmares started.

She tried to shake it all away and took a big bite out of her turkey leg. Wanting to enjoy her lunch, she bathed in the warm sun streaming through the barn's skylight, like one of her many cats. The sound of the horses neighing and muffled voices from below caught Viviana's attention. Knowing the hour was getting late and her father would be worried, she scurried down the nearest ladder. She headed home, hoping not to run into Anthony again. She didn't know if she would be able to control herself this time.

As she headed back to the Manor, she noticed Anthony coming toward her, heading in the direction of town. Her anger flared, growing as he came closer. She wanted to burn him to a crisp. All the hate she had for what he stood for started to heat her palms. Viviana tried desperately to calm herself as he approached her, but nothing was working. She turned away from him and started walking away. *This is ridiculous. You need to control yourself. He is NOT them. Calm down and just talk to him.* She took a breath, turned around and saw his face less than a foot away from hers.

His stone-cold features made Viviana nervous. She could not tell if he was happy or sad or angry. She smiled, hoping he would do the same.

"Anthony, I am glad to see you. I am sorry…"

"I know why you ran again, Viviana, and if it is that hard to be around me, I will leave when my mission is complete," he said frankly. "Until then, I will stay in the inn and not set foot in the Manor." He headed toward town, leaving Viviana to stew for a moment. Nothing would make her happier than him gone, but what about everyone who would miss him being around the Manor? She caught up to him and made him stop.

"You, sir, know nothing about me. The sight of that damn mark...I would be happy if you never had come back here," Viviana looked into his eyes, and he shifted on his feet. He put his head down and looked as if he was going to leave. "But Auntie would be heartbroken if I ran you out of the Manor. I may not like what you are, but I will try to not to hold it against you. You ARE family, after all." She turned on her heels and continued walking. "Just don't get hurt again. I may not be around next time."

Anthony stood there as she strolled into the town's largest inn. She looked back to see him smiling. He stopped when he noticed her looking at him. They froze for a moment when a gruff, husky booming voice called out to them.

"Little Vi, and am I going blind? Is that little Andy?" Bractus squeezed the breath out of each of them.

"Bractus, my old friend, I am glad to see you are still well enough to run this broken-down mule of an inn," Anthony said.

They all laughed at the joke. Sharzet was the most beautiful inn in Dragoonus. The wood tables sparkled, and the floors shined. The hearth held a roaring fire that heated the place. The setting sun's rays danced over the tables and bottles behind the bar. Everyone knew to be on their best behavior and watch how many ales they drank.

23

This place was too pretty to destroy in a bar fight. Plus, Bractus put patrons to bed or out the door before they had the chance to become rowdy.

"So, what brings the mistress of the Manor here to my humble establishment?" he asked gingerly.

"I wanted a drink before heading back to the Manor. I guess my cousin here could have one with me. Maybe share a tale or two?" She smiled at Anthony, who cringed at the mention of alcohol.

"Well, if that is the case," he handed her a bottle of hard apple ale, "the first bottle is on me. Mathilda asked for several cases of my best rum, so I guess the ale ought to be a good starter for the night." He smiled as he retrieved a glass for Anthony.

"Thanks, I think," he said, holding the bottle and rolling his eyes at Viviana.

"What? The boys will drink you under the table if you don't start now."

"'Drunkenness dulls the senses and makes strong men weak' to quote my old master. I try not to indulge too often. Have you, cousin? You do not look old enough to have had your first glass," he asked with one eyebrow raised.

"You would ask such a bold question of a lady? Then again, I guess most around here don't consider me a lady," she giggled at the look on Anthony's face. He gave her a half-smile and shook his head.

"You need a haircut and a shave, cousin," Viviana said. "I am surprised that Auntie let you out of the Manor."

"I didn't give her a chance. Last time, she almost killed me. Blood was everywhere. Then I let her cut my hair and I looked like my father. I didn't want to leave my room." He smiled at her.

24

"When were you here last?" she asked.

"About three years ago," he said while looking around the inn.

"Three years ago? Why didn't I…" she thought a moment, "unless you came while I was away at the University. But no one ever mentioned it." She looked at him, but he avoided her eyes.

"It was right before that, but you were busy getting ready to leave. Plus, I was here on business," he said looking into her eyes. She shivered. "Are you cold?" he asked with concern.

"No, just caught a chill from the breeze. So, what business did you have here then?"

"I was trying to leave the Capitol. Guarding royalty is a pain and dangerous. I always wanted to be a scholar, but no matter how much I enjoy learning, I am better with a sword than a pen." He started walking to the door with the bottle in his hand. "Maybe tonight I will let go and drink." He was trying to change the subject.

"So, I guess you had to go back to being a guard?"

"Once a guard…couldn't really get out, especially when the king…" He stopped and shook his head. "Sorry, there are things I know that no one can."

"So why are you back now and why were you being attacked? Does it have to do with the revolution?" Her curious eyes met his.

He shook his head again. "I really cannot explain what happened. Your father swore me to secrecy, and I cannot break my word."

"Ah, well I will talk to him then. I have my own ways of gathering information." She smiled and headed out of the inn with Anthony on her heels. They walked three shops down and entered. The smell of sweet spices and flowers greeted them, and Anthony's eyes widened.

25

The store was a salon of beauty, where women of all types came to clear their skin and style their hair. All the women in the room turned to see Viviana and they started talking to her at once. The chatter stopped when they noticed Anthony behind her. Mrs. Cauldrius was the first to speak.

"My girl, what beastly creature followed you here?" she teased, knowing full well who he was.

"Oh, you know how it goes. They give you the puppy dog eyes, and you just can't say no," she said smiling. "This puppy needs a shave horribly," she shook her hand at his hair.

"So now I am a shaggy dog?" he asked, playfully. She gave him a look that made him straighten up a little and he marched over to the chair. She was holding back a lot of anger because he was not the enemy, however, the embers of hate still lingered and if he added fuel, then he would get burned.

"I guess I shouldn't object to a cut and shave?" he asked, as he sat in the chair.

"Nope, and while you are getting pretty, I am going back to the house. I am sure Auntie is worried about her baby boy. I should report that you are going to actually look decent for the party tonight."

"Well, if there is a party, I should do your hair Vi. You really need something beautiful, something Calestius. A trader came to town with some pictures of a hairstyle that would suit your beautiful face," Mrs. Cauldrius said, trying to guide her to a chair.

"Father will be furious with me if I do my hair again, and besides, it's Anthony's party. I want him looking his best," she giggled and waved goodbye as she left the shop. She enjoyed the thought of him in that shop with all those chatty women. He did need a shave and a cut, and Mrs. Cauldrius was the best for both women and men.

Once back at the Manor, she went to find her father. He would be the best source for information.

"Hello, father," she said giving him a hug and kiss as he sat in his favorite chair by the fireplace. He motioned for her to sit down by him and looked deep into her sapphire eyes.

"Is Anthony okay?" he asked. There was so much concern in his voice it unsettled her, but she kept her composure.

"Don't worry about him. He is in the hands of Mrs. Cauldrius. I decided to treat him to a cut and shave. He was looking so dreadful and shaggy, so I thought it might be nice for him to look decent for the party tonight." She picked up an apple from the fruit bowl and took a bite.

"Besides," she wiped the juice from her mouth, "he is family. I just have to get to know him and work on my calming technique. I haven't hurt him yet, and I hope I can continue. Just tell him to keep his mark covered. It is still too painful to see." She stood from the table.

"I will tell him. I am proud of you; you have done so well. Just remember, if you start to feel unrest in your heart, run. And keep running, the farther away from people you are, the better for us all." He sighed and put his hand on her head. "I am so sorry, my dear, that you have such powerful abilities."

"It's a curse. I know I can help so many people, but I can hurt so many, too. It's like I'm one of those witches from the fairy tales mother used to tell me. They would cause so much chaos and try to ruin the princess' life."

"Until a handsome prince rescued her…"

"No. The princess would save the day by making the evil witch come to her senses." She smiled, remembering

27

how her mother would act out the scenes for her. "Mother knew that I had to keep my 'evil witch' in check. No one else can save me, but me." She took his hand from her head and held onto it.

"You've grown so quickly. Why can't you just be my little girl a little longer?" He looked into her sapphire eyes.

"I wish I could be too, but my powers are just getting worse. That's why I would like to visit the Calestius Sun Shrine and study there. Homer said that is where the calming technique was invented. Supposedly, this gift is so rare that even Homer was surprised by it." Tears started to well in her eyes. "Why, father? Why was I cursed with this…"

He stopped her with a bear-like hug and rubbed her back, like he used to when she was a small child. Mathilda stepped from the kitchen, and when she saw Viviana crying her face dropped.

"Where is Anthony? Is he okay?" Mathilda asked. Her eyes filled with tears and her lip quivered.

Viviana nodded. "He is fine, Auntie. I promise. He is getting pretty for his homecoming party tonight."

Viviana pulled herself from her father and into the arms of her aunt, the woman who was almost like her mother. After her mother, Ambrosiana, passed away when she was twelve, Aunt Mathilda filled the void. Viviana hated to think she could cause any pain to this wonderful woman.

Mathilda nodded, breathing a sigh of relief. "You just scared me, with the crying and all. Please forgive me." Her aunt hugged her tightly. "Now come help me in the kitchen. There is no homecoming party for Anthony, it is Adilynn's engagement dinner, or did you forget?"

Viviana slapped a hand to her forehead. "Oh no, that's the feast tonight. I thought since Anthony came back...I will be there..." She turned to her father. He nodded and she left with her aunt.

Viviana scampered off to the kitchen behind Mathilda. She knew she needed training and her family could only protect her from the evils of the world for so long.

Chapter 4

The kitchen was warm from the bread baking in the gigantic stone fireplace. Viviana saw the massive feast Mathilda was preparing and knew the whole town would be at her home tonight. She walked around, examining the gigantic cake iced with creamy frosting, and the towers of cupcakes. The meat would be bison and several chickens. Mathilda's chicken was the best. It was always tender and fell from the bone. The herbs and seasonings were fresh from the garden and their fragrance mixed with the sweet-smelling desserts.

"Auntie, this feast is amazing. I guess we invited the whole town to tonight's party?"

"No, just some select townspeople who are important to us. This feast is mainly for the groom's family." She checked the bread. The aroma made Viviana's stomach growl.

"Is that your stomach? It sounded like a small dog was growling at me," Mathilda said, laughing. She pointed to some fresh bread and cheese. "Eat that and go help your cousin get ready. The guests will arrive soon."

Viviana rolled her eyes dramatically and stomped off toward her room. Mathilda laughed and smacked Viviana's bottom. It was something that she had done since she was a little girl. She always loved helping her aunt and cousin, but she enjoyed making a big deal out of it, stomping off or huffing away like they were an inconvenience to her. After all, she was the Lord's daughter and should be spoiled. However, Viviana never saw herself any different from any other person in the town. She had helped almost every shopkeeper and workman with their trades. She helped roof a home, watched sheep with the shepherds, and cleaned out the stables at the Manor. Working side by side with the townspeople gave her a deep respect for all she had in life. They were the reason she did not have to work to live.

With her plate and cup of cider, she made her way to her cousin's room. As she turned the corner, she heard muffled cries. Viviana found her cousin face down in a pillow, her body shuddering with sobs. Looking around the room, she saw clothes strewn about and the closet almost bare.

"Sweetie, what's wrong?" she asked as she sat her things down and stroked Adilynn's hair. Her cousin looked up at her and tried to speak, but no words came from her mouth. She swallowed and sniffled.

"I am so scared, Vi! I have only met his parents once, and he has been away at the University for this past year. What if he doesn't love me anymore? What if he doesn't think I am pretty?" Adilynn blotted her face with the bedding. Her eyes were puffy, and her dress was crumpled. Viviana grabbed a brush from the vanity and returned to her cousin's side, sitting behind her, and gently brushing her hair.

31

"Remember how the boys used to chase you at the University?" Viviana smiled and sipped her cider.

"Oh, you mean both of us? You had several suitors try to talk you into marriage," Adilynn teased.

"Well, it was you who actually said yes to someone. None of those men knew me, just that I was the daughter of a wealthy lord. You, on the other hand, had a man literally fall for you." They both laughed, remembering how Adilynn had met Euclid. He was going to school to become a scholar and teacher, but was well known for his horse-riding skills. He could out-ride anyone from any place in the world, so he said.

"He looked too pitiful laying there on the ground. I couldn't believe that he saw me and just poof… he was on the ground before I could blink. He swears to this day that it was my beauty that blinded him and his horse. That's why the horse bucked and threw him to the ground. I ran over and kept the horse from killing him." Adilynn's face lit up remembering that day.

"He hurt his ankle if I remember right," Viviana said and stepped back to admire the work she did on her cousin's hair.

"Yes, he did. I think you healed him, with that touch of yours, too. His pain was gone so quickly." She looked in the mirror and smiled.

"Well, it was a simple fix. I didn't need much power to heal him." Viviana loved to see her cousin's beautiful smile.

"I just wish his friends wouldn't have made such a deal out of us helping him. It was such a romantic moment," she sighed.

"Well, I am just happy that Euclid isn't like those other pigheaded boys." Viviana found a new dress for her and helped her change. Leading her to the looking glass, she put a fresh coat of blush and lip color on her. She was looking more and more beautiful as Viviana did everything she could to calm her down.

"He is a wonderful man. I am so in love with him, and from his letters, he is still very much in love with me. I just hope the year away will not make things awkward for us tonight. Speaking of who is your date, Vi?" The question caught Viviana off guard, and she choked on her cider.

"Date? I didn't know I had to have one. I don't have anyone for tonight, but I don't think that will be a problem since I am escorting you downstairs. I'll just disappear into the kitchen until dinner is ready. This is your night."

"What about Gavius? He still has a thing for you." Adilynn smiled.

"No, we are just friends. I had a little crush on him, but I am almost twenty-one years old, and he is just too immature for me. Besides, I want to continue my studies at the University and the Sun Shrine. I think learning is the best thing I can do with my time. Marriage and children, I leave to you." She bowed to her cousin.

Viviana would never tell her she was afraid of dying an old maid. Love was never meant for her. She felt nothing for Gavius. He had every girl in town falling for him, anyway. Unlike Euclid, Gavius *was* the pigheaded type. And an arrogant bastard. She drank the rest of her cider, feeling her insides warming.

"Okay. Well, let us get you dressed, Vi. I know the perfect outfit. I don't think mother would be upset if I got into the closet," Adilynn said.

She headed for the second closet in her room, the special closet, meant for only the finest and most expensive outfits the women of the Manor owned. They all were about the same size, except Viviana was much

33

more endowed in the bust. That was only a problem with the newer gowns from Calestius. Adilynn pulled out a satin, sapphire blue dress.

"This will bring out your eyes," she said to Viviana.

"No gown you put on me will take anyone's eyes from you, cousin," Viviana said as she put the dress on. "You are the most beautiful woman in this town, and I am sure that Euclid will be fighting off every man not related to you tonight," she giggled.

Viviana peered into the looking glass and was taken aback by how the dress hugged her figure. The ruffles covered just the tops of her shoulders, and the gown ended right above her ankles. The neckline showed much more skin than her father would approve of. She did not care. She looked stunning, but there was something missing.

Viviana told her cousin she would be back and walked down to her room to find the diamond necklace her mother left her. The sparkling gem made her heart sing in delight as it hung right above her cleavage. Her mother told her this necklace was given to her by Queen Loviana before she left the palace. This was Viviana's most prized treasure. She put it on and looked at herself in the mirror. *Much better.*

After making their grand entrance, the girls headed over to Lord Bion. As expected, he was stunned by Viviana's attire, but said nothing. He knew she was as stubborn as her mother, and just as beautiful. As they chatted and mingled with the guests, Viviana heard a familiar voice behind her.

"Is that liquid courage?" Gavius said.

With a roll of the eyes, Viviana turned to him. He was dressed well for a blacksmith's son. The mead-colored suit jacket did not quite fit his broad shoulders and stout frame, but nothing could detract from his sparkling hazel eyes and chiseled jawline. He smiled and hugged Adilynn and then Viviana, lingering a little too long for her liking. She pushed him away.

"Sorry, sweetie," he whispered while brushing a loose strand of hair away from her face. Viviana smacked his hand away from her and turned from him. He smiled and moved to take her arm, but she did not give him the chance. She didn't want him to get the wrong impression, so she moved over to her father. A touch on her shoulder caused her to turn. Her father smiled down at her and held a handout to a couple she didn't recognize.

"Viviana," he started, "may I introduce you to Euclid's parents, Mr. and Mrs. Greenfield."

She bowed to them and smiled. Her father then waved over a tall, portly man. "And this young man is Euclid's older brother, Turshius. You might have met him at the University."

Viviana glared. "Yes, we have met before. If you will excuse me, I am needed in the kitchen," she said, trying to bow out from the group gracefully.

"A daughter of a lord should never be in the kitchen," Turshius said with a slimy grin. "Are they not the hostesses of parties and such?"

Anger boiled within her. *Who the hell did he think he was?* Somehow, she swallowed the words she really wanted to say and simply smiled.

"Well, this is my cousin's party. She is the hostess tonight. Besides, in this Manor, we are all family, and no one is beneath doing whatever needs to be done. Goodnight."

She curtsied and walked away, not allowing Turshius another word. She sped through the crowd towards the kitchen, stopping when she noticed Anthony. He was gorgeous! His features were much more striking without all that hair on his face. His short, curly hair made him look younger than when she first saw him. She jumped when someone bumped into her.

"Who are you staring at?" Adilynn whispered in her ear.

Viviana put a hand on her chest. "Don't frighten me like that. I just saw your brother all cleaned up! I didn't recognize him for a moment. He really is as handsome as you are beautiful."

"You have no idea how many eyes are on you tonight, Vi." She pointed to a small group of men. They all tried to hide the fact that they were looking at the two of them, but their sidelong glances gave them away.

"They only want me for my father's title and money," Viviana said. "He is the wealthiest lord in Dragoonus. Besides, I just don't find any of them attractive, especially," she motioned to Euclid's brother, "that one."

She shivered at the thought of him. He tried to court Viviana back at the University, but his barbaric ideas of what a woman was good for did not make for fun conversation.

"Well, I doubt your father will arrange anything, at least not for another year," Adilynn said with a smile.

Viviana didn't smile. It made her sick thinking about arranged marriages. That archaic practice normally appealed only to the highest-ranking nobility. Her father married her mother, a lady-in-waiting to the queen's sister, after meeting her while visiting the capital of Dragoonus. They always made their story sound so normal, but to Viviana it was the most romantic love story ever. That was the only story she sought. She was a little envious that Adilynn found her happy ending, but would want nothing less for her sweet cousin.

The girls discussed the size of the cake when Euclid appeared. His sandy blonde hair was shorter than his shoulders and tucked behind his ears. His suit was tailored and fit his well-trimmed body perfectly. No one would ever assume he and Turshius were brothers. He bowed to Viviana and then scooped up his blushing bride-to-be in a warm embrace.

"Euclid, we are in public," she said and pretended to pull herself away.

"Everyone knows we will be wed in one week. That means I can do this," he kissed her on the hand, "and this," he kissed her on the neck, "and of course, this!" He kissed her sweetly on the lips.

"Euclid, enough. You are making me sick," Viviana said, hitting him lightly on the arm. Euclid flinched like she hurt him, then he smiled and kissed her on the cheek. He was like the brother she always wanted. Not only was he funny, sweet, and charming but also could be quite annoying.

"Well, soon-to-be cousin, if you would just find yourself a man…" he said, pointing to the same group of men Adilynn showed her.

"No thank you. Especially not from over there. The University has accepted women as intellectual equals and will allow me to complete a degree. I could become a teacher or finish my training to become a traveling healer. I could do great things without a man attached to me." She grabbed a drink and held it up like she was making a toast before taking a swig of the sweet honey wine.

"There is a man out there for you, Vi. You just need to look and stop being so negative," Adilynn said while giving her a hug.

"Thanks, Addy," Viviana said, laughing.

She knew Adilynn meant well, but she just didn't understand. Viviana was not planning on ever getting married. Her mother told her that the right man was very hard to find, that God was smiling on her mother when she met her father. Their story was what Viviana wanted with all her heart, but she knew those stories were very rare. She was not holding her breath for her handsome, caring, dashing prince to come sweep her off her feet.

"So, do we have tents if it starts to rain?" Euclid said, trying to change the subject.

"Oh, no! I don't know if mother got the tents." Adilynn started to panic.

"Calm down. We have plenty of places where... wait, who is that?" Viviana pointed at a person over by her father. Adilynn told her he was the minister who would perform the wedding ceremony. He came all the way from the University as a favor to Lord Bion. They went to school together, and he was the best in his profession. She wondered why he looked familiar. While lost in thought, she heard Anthony's voice behind her.

"So, Euclid, it's been a while. You still want to settle for my sister?" Anthony nudged him in the ribs with his elbow. Euclid grabbed Adilynn around the waist and grinned.

"What do you mean, settle?" Adilynn hit Anthony on the arm.

"Children, how many times do I have to tell you to behave in public?" Mathilda said, walking up to the group.

"At least once more. mother," they said in unison, and both laughed. Mathilda rolled her eyes at them and took Adilynn's arm, guiding her away from the group to the kitchen.

"So, you are here for the wedding, Anthony?" Euclid asked, raising a brow.

"Yes, I was able to get away from my duties until after the grand day," he said, taking a swig of his mug.

"Ah look! The mighty Anthony has graced us all with his presence again. Tell me, what are you doing back here? How did one of the mad king's precious mongrels get off the leash?" Gavius, with a cup of some potent smelling drink in his hand, wobbled up to the group. The stench made Viviana sick, and she stepped away from him.

"What are you doing?" Viviana growled at him.

Gavius's glare fixed on her. "What are you doing with the king's dog?"

"Gavius," Anthony sighed, "nice to see you again."

"What has gotten into you?" Adilynn appeared from the kitchen with a basket of warm, fresh tarts in her hand.

"Your brother is a traitor and will bring down the resistance with his lies. There is no way…" Gavius stopped his ranting when a large hand landed solidly on his shoulder.

"Young Mr. Black, this is a festive occasion. There will be no talk of such things here. Do you understand?" Lord Bion squeezed Gavius' shoulder. His eyes were filled with anger. He did not want anyone to ruin the party, especially with so many people here who were not involved with their plans.

Lord Bion guided Gavius away from the group, and the remaining four just stared at each other. Adilynn motioned for Viviana to follow her as she headed away from the men.

"What was Gavius talking about?" Viviana asked Adilynn.

"Anthony came here to give your father information about the king's condition. They say that the same madness that took the first king is upon his brother. He is trying to get rid of the High Council and all his advisers. He has talked about gaining support from foreign barbaric countries and there's a rumor of war with Calestius."

All these things Viviana had heard while eavesdropping; however, she still wondered why Gavius would accuse Anthony of lying to her father, the leader of the resistance.

"What does Gavius have against your brother?" she asked. Adilynn rolled her eyes and huffed.

"That goes back to when Gavius was trying to become a knight himself. Anthony was accepted not only into the academy but also the king's knight apprenticeship. Gavius wasn't accepted into either. He's still bitter about that. I think Gavius feels like the second best when Anthony is around. The only thing that Gavius is good at is shoeing a horse and looking handsome."

The girls walked to the end of the dining hall together and greeted Euclid's parents. They were farmers who did all they could to give their sons a future far away from the fields. Their attire was modest, but suitable for the occasion. They spoke about the details of the wedding and what would happen once the ceremony was over.

Adilynn was commenting on where they would live during Euclid's professorship at the University when a series of angry shouts were heard near the kitchen. They ran over and found Anthony holding Gavius by the arms, trying to talk some sense into him. It didn't do any good. He kicked Anthony in the groin, causing him to double over in pain. Gavius then punched him in the face and knocked him to the ground. Viviana wanted to run to Anthony's side and help him up, but he was not down long enough for that. He picked himself up, growled, and ran at Gavius. Anthony dodged a punch and slammed him to the ground, pinning him there.

Gavius wiggled one arm free and grabbed at Anthony, ripping his shirt sleeve. Viviana's pulse quickened when she saw Anthony's arm. The Mark. She let out a hiss, the anger overflowing within. Just as she prepared to strike, a shout from behind made her pause.

"Viviana!" Her father's voice rang in her ears.

Somehow, she remembered his command to run. Summoning every ounce of strength, she fled. Past the party and down the hallway. Her legs took her closer and closer to the door leading to the town. A town full of people.

Chapter 5

Viviana made her way from the dining hall towards the front door. She could feel her skin pulsating with heat. Resting her hand on the stone wall, it glowed with an unnatural red light. Her body grew heavy, and she sat down. Hearing someone running towards her, she turned and saw him.

Her sapphire eyes now burned with a golden-red hue, like looking into the sun. She flung herself at him with impossible speed and grabbed his upper arms. He cried out in pain as she burned his skin with her hands. He tried to pull away from her.

"VIVIANA," he screamed. He yelled out again as her hand gripped his arm tighter.

"Anthony!" Lord Bion exclaimed from down the hall.

Viviana blinked at hearing her father's voice, and her eyes faded to sapphire again. She looked at Anthony and then at his arms. Releasing him, she took two steps back and stumbled. Her head spun. *What have I done?*

"Viviana!" her father cried out as Anthony leapt to catch her just in time to keep her head from hitting the stone floor. He slid to the ground with Viviana's dead weight. She was unconscious in his lap.

A sharp stab brought his attention back to his arm. The pain from Viviana's touch was more intense than any of the wounds he received before. It felt as if the heat melted his flesh and muscles together.

He sat waiting for Lord Bion and Mathilda to catch up. Lord Bion went straight to his daughter, checking her pulse. Tending to her son, Mathilda silently wept tears of joy and anger.

"My sister, please take care of your idiot son," Lord Bion said as he left Anthony in his mother's care.

"You ran right into a wasp's nest! What were you thinking?" she said, helping him to his feet. Anthony shook his head with a shrug. They walked down the hall to the healing house on the other side of the Manor. Mathilda placed the cooling salve on his arms and bandaged them.

"Here, take this," she said while handing him a small vial of liquid.

"I can take the pain. I hate that foul-tasting medicine and it makes me queasy."

"Take it on your own or I will call for your father to help me, just like when you were little." She smiled when he grabbed the vial and gulped the medicine down. He made a face as if she made him eat a whole lemon. Anthony then lay there on the table and in a matter of minutes, he was snoring.

The next morning, Anthony awoke to see Viviana at his bedside. He sat up and tried to say something, but she started before he could.

"I tried to stop, but… I couldn't." Viviana looked as if she was going to cry.

He reached out and placed a hand on hers. "I caused you so much pai—"

"It's not your fault. Gavius is to blame. We won't have to worry about him anymore. They banned him from the Manor."

Viviana huffed in frustration. "Gavius is a love struck fool hell-bent on winning my hand. It's no secret he doesn't like you."

Anthony grunted. "It's not *my* fault he's a terrible knight."

"I don't think he cares. I hope he just disappears." She offered him a smile, but Anthony would still not look at her. Her eyes fell on his bandages, and she breathed deeply.

"But now you're doing better… with the salve I made you?" Viviana bit her lip nervously. He nodded and placed his hand over the bandages. She wanted to see the damage but was frightened by the mark.

"I need to redress your arms. Hopefully they are not too damaged," she said as she worked on his left arm. As she wiped away the salve, Viviana could see the burn was almost healed. *Thank goodness.*

"Vi, you don't have to do the other arm. I will call for mother…" He tried to move away from her.

Viviana raised her hand to silence him. "I have to do my duty, and that is taking care of you. I caused the damage. I have to fix it." She took a deep breath and removed the bandage.

"Wow," Anthony said. "Open your eyes, Vi." She slowly opened one, but the other quickly followed at what she saw. His right bicep no longer showed the king's mark. It now glowed with the bright red print of Viviana's hand. She hesitantly touched the skin.

"Does it hurt?" she asked.

"It just throbs a little," he said.

She looked up at him. "It's hot."

He nodded, holding her gaze.

She wouldn't say it out loud, but she felt better now that the mark was gone. Unfortunately, that symbol was replaced by another—hers. On him for life, forever a reminder of her anger. His hand settled on hers, forcing her to look up again.

"I would much rather wear your handprint than the bastard king's mark, my sweet cousin," he said as he took her hand and kissed it sweetly. She blushed. Looking into his eye, she saw them twinkle in delight. "Besides, I got to punch Gavius one more time last night. I would endure your wrath a thousand times over to do that again." He grinned from ear to ear as he got out of bed and put on his shirt and boots.

Viviana watched as he strode away as if nothing had happened. She sighed. *How long can I go on like this? I must get help.*

"I need to go find father," she said, rising from her chair.

Anthony reached for the door and held it open for her. He smiled as she approached him. Her cousin had suffered at her hands, but he did not hold it against her. This man was not the enemy. She smiled with the feeling of calm as he walked up to her.

"Do you need anything before I go?" She stared into his eyes.

He shook his head. "No, I'm fine. As much as I hate to admit it, Mother's potions do the trick. They taste foul, but they are effective."

She smiled. "As effective as they can be against me."

"Well," Anthony knelt to grab his boots. "Let's just say I'm staying on your good side from here on out."

"Good idea. Now I will see you later at dinner. Stay out of trouble." They nodded and parted ways.

She headed to her father's favorite spot, the war room, and found him looking at the map on the wall, rubbing his temples, looking frustrated or worried, she wasn't sure.

"Father, why are you staring at the map?" Viviana asked quietly, not to startle him. He smiled at her and beckoned her to his side.

"Oh, my dove, you are so curious. This is a good sign. You will be an outstanding leader someday, my daughter. I suppose you should know what is happening. You're just as involved as the rest of us. Your cousin brought us news that the bastard king is trying to annex land to make a new empire."

"An empire? So, it can crumble like the last one? Hasn't he read the history archives?"

"He needs soldiers. The king knows the people are not happy but refuses to fix the underlying problems of greed and corruption in the Capitol. Our leader is also obsessed with power. He will stop at nothing to unite the two kingdoms under his reign. I have a way of stopping him, but this is not the time yet." He looked at the map again.

She recognized the outlines of the kingdom of Dragoonus before the new king started gaining ground close to Calestius. The small kingdoms were part of the rebellion against the rule of the Dragoonus Empire over five hundred years ago. After the empire fell, two large kingdoms were created, Calestius and Dragoonus, and small pockets of tribal groups took their land back from the invaders. These groups kept peace with the larger kingdoms and could have their own government without interference.

"How?" Viviana wanted to know.

"I cannot tell you yet. The less you know, the better protected you are. There are people out there who are looking for an opportunity to break up the resistance before we can get more support behind us. Right now, we are trying to get Calestius to stand with us, but our trade routes would be cut off with them if they tried to stand against the king. I want you to promise me something, Vi." He looked deep into her eyes. "On your birthday, I am sending you to the Sun Shrine to study and train. Promise me you will stay there until I send for you. If I never send for you, then you stay in Calestius. The queen owes me a favor, and she will keep you safe."

"But what about the journey? I won't be safe until I get to Calestius."

"I'm sending Anthony with you."

"Why do I need HIM? Why do I need anyone to look after me? I am not a child!" Viviana could feel the anger rising again and she closed her eyes. She needed to stay calm.

"I charged him as a young boy to guard you with his life. He only became a knight to learn information about the rebellion and how to better protect you."

"Why?" she asked. This news made little sense to her.

"I needed someone I could trust with your life by your side. You are too precious to me and will soon have your own role to play in this fight. You must be ready for that time." He held her against him and kissed her gently on the top of her head. Bion looked down to see her

47

wiping tears from her eyes and hugged her harder until she pulled away.

"Sorry. I am… Father, my birthday is two weeks away. Couldn't we leave with the wedding party to have more protection?"

Lord Bion blinked. "It's a fine idea, but…" his eyes dropped in sadness, "I wanted to celebrate your twenty-first birthday."

Viviana's heart sank. "It's okay. I can stay. I'm sure Anthony and I will…"

Lord Bion shook his head. "No, you're right. The more protection we have for you, the better. After the wedding, you will leave with the caravan and travel to the border with Euclid's family. You must then cross over and be swift; you will travel into Calestius as fall turns to winter. The snow will make your journey difficult. I will send a message to Euclid's father." He suddenly smiled. "I am so proud to be your father, Viviana. You are so special."

As he hugged her again, she glanced at the map, at her next task. The journey would stretch over two kingdoms with treacherous terrain. The quickest route was along a trade road known to occupy both merchants and thieves. Even knowing the danger, Viviana still wished to travel to the Sun Shrine and learn all she could about herself and her powers. Now more than ever. The ringing of the dinner bell turned her attention from the map to her stomach. Lord Bion slid her from his lap and stood.

"Come," he said. "It's time for dinner."

Chapter 6

A light shimmered in Viviana's window as she sat at her desk. She eyed the stack of books she carried from her father's study. They were thick and worn on the edges. Handwritten accounts of centuries lay within the pages, and she wanted to understand more about these divided kingdoms once belonging to one country.

She tried to focus as she opened the first book. According to the manuscript, Princess Loviana of Calestius married Dragoonus' last ruler, King Demosthenes, after his previous wife passed away. Their union produced a daughter, Auriana Cleopatra Viviana, but the marriage failed soon after the child's second birthday. From the official records, the king caught Queen Loviana with another man and sentenced her to death. Fleeing to Calestius with her daughter, the queen lost the princess to a terrible accident. Stricken with grief, the queen fell ill and locked herself away in the Sun Shrine of Calestius. The king passed away weeks later of an unknown illness.

The only picture Viviana had seen of their family convinced her that the king was the father of the child. At the age of two, the princess had the king's nose and chin. She also had her mother's beautiful dark auburn hair and heart-shaped face.

All her reading reminded her of the information gained from a friend, and she was due to visit him again. Not just to verify the information; Viviana wanted to tell him she was leaving and had to go during the midnight bell, when the stable boys were sleeping.

Her thoughts drifted to the journey ahead. Leaving made her uneasy, but she knew she had to go. She needed to control her powers if she was going to be of any use in the rebellion. And she needed to be away from Dragoonus. Her emotions were unstable; at any moment she could snap again. She had to protect the ones she loved.

Silently, Viviana put on her riding shoes and cloak. After grabbing a basket, she filled it with pastries, bread, and fruit. She quickly put out the candle and took the hidden passageway to the stables. Viviana paused before coming out from the protection of the hidden panel by the horse stalls. She heard voices, familiar voices.

"Yes, she will be here momentarily. You should go now if you want to make it to the woods before her. You can hide in the caves by the river."

"I will not hide. I am going to be by her side," a male voice replied.

It was Adilynn and Anthony, but what were they doing there? Viviana opened the panel enough to crawl through. Ducking into a stall, she watched as Adilynn handed her brother a small leather satchel.

"He is not friendly to men, especially young ones. You won't be safe." She helped him fasten his cloak around his shoulders.

"Then I'll ask Lord Bion for more men."

"There is no one who would willingly venture into that area of the woods with you. The townspeople believe it to be haunted."

"Since when?" Anthony looked puzzled.

"Since Lord Bion pledged to protect his area of the woods from townspeople so that he can hunt and live in peace. Remus is committed to keeping Viviana safe. In his own way, he cares for her."

Anthony grunted at her. "I am her protector, and if she gets hurt, not only will Lord Bion kill me, but the resistance will also be in jeopardy. I cannot keep her safe if I do not know what that beast is."

"There is nothing you need to protect her from in those woods. She is quite capable. The thing that should worry us is what we all will have to face soon. I knew our family had its fair share of secrets, but this one…" Viviana moved the door open a fraction more and tried to see their faces.

She heard Anthony say, "… could destroy the fabric of our family and…" before her a horse let out a loud grunt.

"Who's there?" Anthony took out his sword.

They gaped at her when she stepped out into the open.

Viviana scowled. "Happy to see you, too."

"Why were you eavesdropping on us?" Adilynn said.

"I was not doing it on purpose. I came out here to get Moonkiss and ride to see Remus. What are *you* doing here?" She looked at Anthony. "And you aren't coming with me. Remus will kill you. And what have you been hiding from me? What secrets do you have?"

Again, they looked at each other before Anthony took a gentle step toward her.

"We are not related, Viviana."

"What?" Viviana and Adilynn said together.

"We are not related by blood." He looked away from her.

"Then… how are we related?" She looked at Adilynn.

"Please sit, Vi." She guided her over to a small bench. "Mathilda and Marcus adopted us. So, in a way, we are still cousins."

"Our actual parents died right after Adilynn was born," Anthony said. "Mathilda had them brought in when a horrible sickness swept through here. We survived, but we were orphans, and Mathilda couldn't have children."

"I had no idea," Viviana said.

"We have known only for a short time ourselves. Since Marcus is a third born son, he does not need a blood heir for a lordship. Lord Bion approved the adoption and sealed the papers away in the family vault."

"Why?"

"The wedding," Adilynn piped in. "Our parents had to tell Euclid's parents about the relationship as part of the marriage agreement, but our family wanted to protect us." She took Viviana's hands. "It doesn't matter if we are adopted or not. You're my cousin, no matter what."

Viviana threw her arms around Adilynn. "Absolutely! You are my best friend. Blood makes no difference to me. Why were you worried about telling me?"

"Because I love you like a sister, and I was worried you would be uncomfortable with Anthony as your guardian." Adilynn wiped away her tears.

"He is family. That is not my reason for being uncomfortable with him. I am trying to keep myself in check, but he is still a knight." She looked at him and sighed. Her heart was still torn about him. A part of her wanted to trust him and felt he was a valiant knight, like in the storybooks, but another part of her still wanted to set him on fire.

"I swear to you my allegiance is to this family and no one else." He went down to one knee and placed his sword at her feet. "My life is yours, Viviana. Where you go, I will go, and no harm will come to you on my watch. This I swear." Her heart skipped a beat when he looked up at her. Never had a man pledged himself to her, and it made her flustered. She motioned him to stand.

"Please, I am going out tonight to see Remus and I must get going," Viviana said. "He will be sad that I am leaving, but I asked my father to find another friend for him. Coryn has met him before and she seemed quite taken with him." Viviana smiled as she saddled Moonkiss.

"I am coming with you, Vi," Anthony said before she finished with her horse.

"If you must, but please do as Adilynn told you. Stay out of sight. I will let him know of your presence, and it is up to him whether he wants to meet you."

"As you wish," he bowed slightly.

Viviana was both elated and saddened by what she'd learned about her cousins. The fact everyone hid this information from her made her mad. Why couldn't they trust her with it? Her father knew and didn't tell her. What was the reasoning behind it all? She wondered what other

53

secrets were lurking in the darkness of her family's past. Pushing them to the side, she looked into the eyes of her horse, her beloved Moonkiss, whose coat was black as night with only a crescent shaped silver patch on his forehead. She stroked his face and whispered instructions to him, which he seemed to understand as he bowed his head.

Viviana and Anthony left on their horses as silent as the stars in the heavens. They made their way to the forest behind the Manor, the barrier between the town and the large hills of the countryside. The magic of the forest comforted Viviana as they rode deeper into the trees.

The caves Remus called home were protected from intruders like a fort. From the items found in there, they were once used as a place for soldiers and commoners to hide during the last rebellion, over a century ago. The cave still had weapons and gear, which were rusty from the moisture of the cave. The mineral-rich pool he once showed her sparkled with gems that may have once decorated the king's soldiers. Viviana took a few of them once, never sharing what she found with anyone. She knew scholars would appear like locusts, and the king would send for the jewels and weapons as trophies. He would find Remus and capture him. No one could know about the caves. She would never forgive herself if he was taken away. *But then, how did Adilynn know about them?* she wondered.

When they reached the cave, Viviana signaled to Anthony to go farther down by the river. He grunted at her, but obeyed her directions. She headed down to the cave of the changeling—the mythical creatures transformed by a venefica, a magical woman who loved to torture men by changing them into beasts. She heard of them only in stories of old, used to scare children to stay out of caves and the deep forests around the Manor.

She had told Anthony of his bear-like body, but his face still had human qualities. His eyes were as pale blue as the sky on a clear winter day. He had the lips and teeth of a man, and his smile was kind and gentle. She did also mention that he was twice the size of Lord Bion and had the strength of ten. Viviana could tell these details did not provide Anthony any comfort for the meeting tonight. He was angry that he had to hide in the caves so far away from her. The creature could do whatever he pleased, and Anthony did not have the speed or strength to protect her.

"Do not worry so much," she said. "He is my friend and has protected me for many years." Viviana recalled how the relationship started after her mother's death. She ran into the forest to hide and cried herself to sleep. She woke in the barn, though could never remember how she made it there. The next day, she found tracks leading to the woods. She followed them and found a creature hiding in a cave deep in the forest. Back then, she truly thought a magical bear had taken home her.

"I still dislike this, but I will follow your command." Anthony bowed to her and left her at the edge of the clearing, close to the cave entrance. She watched as he took his position in the forest with the horses.

"I see my sweet little rose has made it back to the forest. I am happy you came to see me," Remus' voice called out to her as he cooked dinner by the fire.

"My magical beast! You look well, and dinner smells wonderful." She went up to him and he stood to hug her. On his back legs, he was taller than a full-grown man and could reach fruit off the tree with ease. Viviana thought she heard Anthony curse.

The bear sniffed the air. "You have brought a friend with you. It smells like leather and iron. A man?" He frowned at her. "You know I am not fond of men in my forest."

Viviana looked up at her friend. "He is my cousin. He would not let me leave without him." She opened her satchel and set up what she had brought him.

"Your cousin?"

"Can you please meet him? It's quite rude to let him sit out there while we eat." She placed three wooden mugs down and filled them with apple cider.

There was a silent moment as he sniffed the air again. "He may come here and sit with us. There is no threat from this young one. I know him well."

Viviana frowned and cocked her head. "You have met him before?"

"Yes, many moons ago," Remus smiled, and his teeth glowed in the firelight.

"Anthony!" she shouted for him and waved her arms.

He came bounding towards her with this hand on the hilt of his sword.

"Are you..." The air caught in his throat as Remus stood.

"Oh, come now, my shadow, you were never afraid of anything." Anthony blinked. "Shadow? Only one person on this earth called me that and he is dead." Anthony turned to look the beast dead in its piercing, ice-blue eyes. They stared each other down, Viviana's concern growing with each passing moment. Then Anthony went down on one knee and bowed. "Master."

"Rise, knight," the beast said, placing a paw on Anthony's shoulder. "I have not been your master for many years,"

56

Viviana frowned as she looked at the two of them. "Master?"

Chapter 7

"Remus," Viviana started, "you have some explaining to do and you better start now!"

Her look only made the men laugh, but they stopped as they saw how annoyed she became. "All this time you knew I had another cousin, and you said nothing to me! Everyone, even you, has lied to me."

"I am sorry, Vi. I never imagined I would see him again, and honestly, I did not know he was still alive," Remus said.

"So, how do you know each other?" she asked as she stared into the fire.

"The story goes back many more years than I care to admit. I was once a knight for the king, even became a trainer for the younger recruits. In my time, peace was abundant, and everyone loved the king, so the need for us on the battlefield was unnecessary. Shadow came to us shortly after the king and queen had the little princess. He was so smart and very strong. He beat out several other students to be the top of his class. I believe ten other young boys in all. He was eight when they chased the queen out of the kingdom and the little princess was lost. I did everything I could to protect them, but I failed. I am to blame for the child's death."

He turned away from them. Viviana had never seen him like this; he looked about to weep. She wanted to hug him.

"But how is it your fault?" she asked. "It is the king who didn't trust his wife. His jealousy caused the entire problem."

"It was not jealousy," Anthony butted in, also staring at the fire, "but poison that caused the old king's downfall. We found out an elixir meant to heal him rattled his mind and made him weak. In his condition, anyone could have made him think the queen was disloyal to him." Anthony looked at Viviana. "To this day, Queen Loviana still claims to be innocent of any wrongdoing against the king or the crown."

Remus cringed, but sat quietly.

"All these years and my suspicions were correct. I would have never done such a thing with the queen, even though I…" Remus realized he was talking out loud.

Viviana's jaw dropped. "You? You were the one… Is this why you are what you are? Did the king order you to undergo this change?" Viviana fired questions at her woodland protector, and all he could do was bow his head. "Oh Remus, I am so sorry. I shouldn't have pried." She hugged his arm tightly. He smiled and kissed the top of her head.

"They captured me after the queen disappeared," Remus said as he stared into the fire. His eyes were glazed over as he recalled the past. "I remember the king could not actually kill me since we had grown to respect each other. I also saved his life so many times…" He paused and then whispered, "He was my king." He looked up at the heavens and sighed.

"So, how did you end up here?" Viviana asked when he paused.

"Those attempts on his life, I fear, were from his brother. However, I couldn't find the proof against him. The king condemned me to the dungeon for the rest of my life, but his brother had another idea." Remus ground his teeth in anger.

"How could he have done this to you?" Anthony asked.

"He did not. His wife, Lady Raphiana, is a venefica…" Remus trailed off as if lost in thought.

"Wait, SHE is one of those? I thought they were a myth, like in the stories mother used to tell me." She scratched her head.

"They exist, but they are rare. I had no idea until she used her power on me. She takes great pleasure in morphing humans into foul creatures. After King Dethemous died, his brother took the throne. He gave my life over to her." Remus paused again. "Her favorite sport was hunting, and I was meant to be her next trophy." He shivered.

"So how did you escape?" Anthony asked.

"She poisoned me to keep me weak, except on the day I was to be hunted. I worked all night on the bars and finally could escape, but I only had a small head start. They caught up to me, and I was gravely wounded. Luckily, I found a pond just deep enough to submerge myself in and waited until the dogs lost my scent." Remus stopped and yawned.

"It's getting late. We should go." Anthony stretched his body as he stood.

60

"Not yet. Please finish your story, Remus. I did not know what you had gone through." Viviana's eyes glistened with tears as the dying embers of the fire crackled one last time.

"As you wish," he said, and took a breath. "I struggled on until I found the comfort of your father's barn. Your aunt was tending her horse when I found it. She could tell I was not a creature of nature and tended my wounds in secret. Mathilda saved my life. I, in return, promised to stay in the woods and protect the Manor from intruders. The venefica's curse gave me strength to get the job done. It is probably the only good thing to come out of this," he said, looking at Viviana. "And meeting you, of course."

She smiled. "Auntie always said that a protective spirit lived in these woods. I guess she was right."

"Now I can rest, knowing that Anthony will take my place as your protector." Anthony nodded in agreement when Remus looked over.

"That is what they trained me for as a knight and scholar," Anthony said. "I will keep her safe."

"No, your training is for you to protect royalty, and around here, Viviana is the lady of the Manor. She is royalty." He smiled as he saw Viviana blush.

"I am no such thing." She looked at the embers. "My lot in life is of a healer and a weapon. My abilities are growing, and I am dangerous without proper training. That's why I must leave and go to Calestius. I will be safe there, and able to learn techniques to control my powers. Besides, I have always wanted to travel outside these walls and see the other kingdom. Books and stories from merchants are fine for children, but I need to see everything for myself." She stood and stretched her legs.

"I need some water." She went to the small creek behind the cave and took a large drink from the clear, fresh water. Viviana thought she heard murmuring and wondered what Anthony and Remus were talking about. Sneaking into the woods, she could hear Anthony trying to explain something to Remus.

"Viviana is ro…" Anthony said, but Viviana saw him stop when a rabbit sprinted from her location. His eyes followed the trail back to where she was standing, but she darted behind a tree and waited there. She peered with one eye from the tree and could see Anthony staring back into the fire.

"A rose? Yes, she is beautiful and has bloomed into such a fine woman." Remus said as he took a swig of wine.

"Rose? No, she is… a treasure… one sought by the devil." His words seem to trigger something for Remus, and he spat his wine. Viviana scratched her head and was perplexed. *A treasure? A devil?*

"I wonder where Viviana is?" Anthony looked worried. Not wanting them to suspect she heard them, she headed a little deeper into the wooded area and pretend she just came back.

"Those darn blumberry bushes," she exclaimed as she walked back to the fire. "They caught my dress again."

"I thought you went for a drink of water?" Anthony asked her with a serious look on his face.

"I did. I also remembered that the blumberries should be ready for eating," she said as she placed a few in his hands and then offered some to Remus. He looked taken aback by her arrival.

"Remus, you look like you have seen a spirit. Are you feeling well?" Viviana tried to place her hand on his forehead, but he just laughed at her since she could not reach it. He looked at her and his face returned to normal.

"I am fine, little one. I am just… amazed that you are going to train at the Sun Shrine. Will you get to see the queen?"

"Yes. Father said she would be there for a festival."

Remus looked off, a smile touching the corners of his mouth. "She is the most gracious woman you will ever meet. She is so beautiful, too."

"You were in love with her, weren't you?" Anthony asked.

"It's hard not to fall in love with an incantatrix," he said as he patted Viviana on the head.

"A what?"

"It's what men call a woman who has such a draw to them they cannot help but swoon over her. Queen Loviana is such a woman. She is a magician with her healing touch, but you need to trust the person healing you to make it work. So, I assume that the enchanting power goes along with the healing as well. I saw her work her magic on little Andy one time. He took a severe blow to the head by one of our older students."

"Brontez, that bastard," Anthony mumbled as he touched a spot above his left ear.

"I always knew that it was from my mother's side that I received my gift. I just didn't know everyone in Calestius had such abilities," she said, remembering all the things her mother had taught her through the years.

"You saved my life," Anthony said, smiling at her and rubbing his stomach.

Viviana suddenly remembered something. "You never told me if you figured out what attacked you. Father wouldn't tell me much of that night, and since we will leave soon, I should know what to look for if the attacker comes back." Viviana looked into the woods.

"It was some sort of beast. It hit me from behind and knocked me off my horse. I never saw it." He closed his eyes.

Remus suddenly rose and went deeper into the cave. When he came back, he had the remains of something a little larger than a man. The creature's arms were grotesque with the decay of death and the body looked bloated. The smell made Viviana and Anthony gag. He raised the arm close to the firelight, and the two gasped in fright. Anthony leaned forward and examined the hand. The claws protruded from the hand like fingers, but distorted in a way he had never seen before. The limbs were bulky with muscles and covered in hair, like Remus.

"I found this thing a few weeks ago," Remus said. "It was only after I killed it I realized it was another beast... like me. His face showed less humanness, but I knew it was Lady Raphiana's work. She must have sent the hound after you, Anthony, to kill you. I am surprised that more have not shown up."

"They rarely fail. The only reason I'm still alive is because of Viviana." He looked at her. "And with it now dead, it probably never reported its success."

"Still, you are being out in the open like this is dangerous. And it's not like you have made no enemies since returning."

"You mean besides you?"

She ignored him and stood up to pace. She was more worried now about the safety of her town than her own life. If those mongrels from the king came—or more of those creatures—then the town would be in trouble. She needed to get home.

"We will go now," Viviana said, "and talk to father in the morning. He should know you found this creature and that it is dead. However, there is still the possibility the king will send more of these things."

Viviana started packing her things away.

"Your father knows about me being chased and knows that the king may send more," Anthony said. "He has informants all over this land, keeping us aware of the king's movements. We limit the news of my survival to this town only. Euclid's family knows about our situation and is part of the resistance. We do not have to worry about them. You're going to be at the wedding or Adilynn will kill you."

"It might not be the best thing right now."

Anthony stopped her with a hand on her arm. "Viviana. She'll be devastated if we aren't there."

"But the town will be safe. You have to leave, and I need to get to the Sun Shrine. The longer we wait; the more danger my people are in."

"*Our* people…"

She met Anthony's hard, unwavering gaze before pulling away from him and returning to her pack. "You know, I was thinking…"

"A dangerous pastime for you, Vi," Remus chuckled. She rolled her eyes.

"I was thinking you could come with us, Remus." She looked over at him. "You could see if the queen could make you physically human again."

His reaction was a mix of shock and longing. He finally sighed and shook his head.

"I am not ugly enough to pass as a beast, but I do not look like a man either. I would love to come with you, but I am not sure how I could get there. Besides, I do not know if she even has the powers to change me back. I

65

have been in this form for so many years…" He looked at his hands and sighed again.

"I am sure I can figure out a way for you to travel with us. Lord Bion would do anything to help since you have kept me and Adilynn safe playing in the woods for so long." She smiled.

"We will ask Lord Bion tomorrow," Anthony said. He drained the last of the apple cider from his mug and stood. "For now, we must return."

"Be safe little one," Remus said, hugging Viviana. "Anthony, please watch over her since I cannot anymore." He patted him on the shoulder, almost knocking him over.

"Please, Remus, think about what I said." Viviana clung to the massive hand of her friend. He smiled and stroked her cheek tenderly.

"I will, but now you must go. Someone will be missing both of you. Tell Adilynn I love her and wish her happiness on her wedding day."

"Goodbye," Anthony said, and bowed his head to Remus.

Off they rode back to the Manor as swiftly as their horses could carry them. Viviana focused on the horizon, watching the sun's orange hue kiss the sky and the last star disappear. She knew there were four more days until the wedding, and she would need every hour to prepare herself for the upcoming journey. No matter what happened, she must make it to Calestius and soon.

Chapter 8

As they arrived at the stables, the morning bell sounded, and both looked towards the Manor. They quickly removed the saddles and made their way to the kitchen. There, Mathilda greeted them with a fresh pitcher of water and two plates of food. Viviana had a feeling Adilynn told her about their adventure. She loved her family, but her heart was heavy. For so long, she felt her family was unshakable, and she never imagined all the secrets hid in the shadows of the Manor. She looked at her aunt and sighed. *What other secrets were there? What else were they hiding from me?* Her aunt's voice interrupted her thoughts.

"You two go get some rest. I will have someone come get you when lunch is ready." She smiled and shooed them from the kitchen.

"Thank you, mother," Anthony said.

They both kissed her cheek, and Anthony went toward the dining hall as Viviana headed to her room.

When she opened her door, she placed the empty plate on the vanity and pulled back her covers. The smell of clean linens and fresh herbs made her happy—the little things she would miss about her home. Her mind turned to the journey, and she imagined what they would encounter in their travels. As she let herself relax into bed, two questions swirled around in her head. *Why do they need to protect me with secrets? What is my purpose in life?*

Viviana awoke to the sound of the church bell ringing to signal the noon hour. She was still groggy from sleep, but somehow managed to change into clean clothes and head down to the kitchen.

As she passed through the halls, she saw many unfamiliar faces around the Manor. The great dining hall was looking beautiful, with all the orange, yellow, and red tapestries hanging from the walls. Viviana wished she could be excited for the wedding, but knew time was not on her side. She was lost in thought when she heard a voice behind her.

"Miss, one moment please."

She turned to see a handsome young man with a warm smile. He looked similar to the others in the dining room, and she assumed he was with Euclid's family.

"Yes? How may I help..." She could not finish as she felt a stabbing pain in her stomach. The man laughed as he pulled the knife from her. The pain quickly doubled in intensity as she staggered to the wall behind her. She braced herself against it as she covered the wound with her hand to heal herself. The pain eased, but the wound would not close fast enough. She was losing too much blood.

"Father!" she shouted as the immense pain below her ribs intensified again.

"Die, witch!" the man shouted as he lunged towards her to stab her again.

He let out a grunt as they tackled him to the ground. Viviana heard Coryn's voice shout for Lord Bion, and the echo of her cry brought everyone running. Two men grabbed the assassin and pinned him to the ground. The world blurred, and the ground felt as if it was tilting.

Her father roared her name, and he was suddenly in her vision. She looked up at him, his face a picture of pure fear as he held her. Tears were dripping onto her face as he mouthed something to her. But she couldn't hear him. His face became a blur and then nothing.

"No, Viviana. No… no…"

Anthony appeared as they loaded Viviana's limp body onto a stretcher. "Oh no, Viviana…" He looked almost ghostly as they passed by him. He followed his mother, Mathilda, and Lord Bion to the healing house and watched them transfer her from the stretcher to the bed. Both he and Lord Bion stood by while Mathilda went to get her medicines. Viviana hardly looked to be breathing.

"Anthony…"

Lord Bion's low, harsh voice snapped Anthony out of his thoughts, and he looked over.

"I need you to go to the dungeon and find out all you can from the bastard who did this," Lord Bion did not look away from his daughter as he spoke. "Use the potions if you must. I want answers." He gave him a key and pointed to the cabinet.

"Yes, sire. At once." Anthony bowed, took a small satchel from the cabinet, and left for the holding cell.

Anthony made his way down the spiral staircase to the dungeon. His father was the head of the guards and would be there now. As he moved, his swift and steady footsteps made little noise as he arrived at his destination.

"Anthony, what are you doing here?"

"Lord Bion sent me to interrogate the prisoner. I fear he is from the palace."

"I do not know if that is wise. He might know you…"

"I have permission… to use the potions." He showed him what he had in the pouch. His father did not look pleased.

"I don't want that stuff down here. My brother is not in his right mind if he thinks I will use that, even on this garbage." He pointed to the prisoner. Anthony saw the exposed skin and growled at the sight of the King's Mark. The last informant told him there were rumors of an attack on the family. How he got into the Manor was still a mystery. Lord Bion had guards on patrol from his bedroom down to the town.

A shiver ran down Anthony's back. If they were going after Viviana, what did they know about her? Even so, Anthony had been a knight long enough to know what this was. The king was sending a message.

Anthony knew the routine: either the guard returned, or they would send another. He took out the vial and entered the cell, not flinching when Marcus closed and locked the door behind them. Anger welled within Anthony as he looked at the assassin, his head bowed.

Through gritted teeth, Anthony asked, "Why did you attack Viviana?"

Anthony heard the man whisper, "Do as you will."

"That is what I intend to do." He smiled as he placed the vial on the table and sat across from Viviana's attacker. Anthony sat waiting for the man to stir.

"Is the witch dead?" he asked without lifting his head.

"Is that why the King sent you?" Anthony played with the vial on the table. He could see the assassin eyeing the milky white substance in disbelief.

"So, you do know what this is, then. Let's make this easy. You tell me what I want, and I won't use this on you." Anthony smiled when the man raised his head but growled when he spat in his face.

"Do your worst!" the knight snarled at him like a wild animal. Anthony wiped his face and cracked his neck. He was done playing games.

"Why did you go after the Lord's daughter?" He jumped from his seat and grabbed the man's hair. Anthony looked him in the eyes, but the man just stared through him. The knight just smiled at him and said nothing. Anthony let go of the man's hair and then smacked him in the face.

"You will be my little songbird." Anthony turned and grabbed the vial. The knight cringed at the sight of it. "Yes, this is the ghost elixir. Are you sure you do not want to talk?"

"I will tell you nothing! I am loyal to the king!" The knight thrashed as he tried to get out of his bonds. Anthony smacked him again and grabbed his jaw. The man tried to close his mouth, but Anthony got a few drops in and forced him to swallow. The thrashing about, and the man went limp. Then he looked up at Anthony. He noticed a filmy haze over the knight's eyes. It was working.

"Now, what is your name?"

71

"I am Victoris, a King's Guard of the Second Class."

"Who sent you?"

"The king of Dragoonus."

"What is your mission?"

"To kill Lord Bion's daughter so she could not destroy him."

"Destroy him how?"

"He said she would kill him before the next harvest. She would make a plague that would kill many of the crops and then make the people turn against him."

"This is what his dreams told him?"

"Yes," the knight said as he twitched. "Now what's next?" His body contorted as he became pale. The elixir was taking a toll on the prisoner.

"Next is where you go to sleep and forget everything or die. Either way, this ends now." Anthony poured a vial of a clear substance down his throat. He coughed and then his eyes rolled into the back of his head. His father entered and saw the state of the assassin.

"Is he dead?" Marcus asked.

Anthony sighed and cursed. "If he is, they will just send more." He watched as the man started to breathe again. They both sighed with relief.

"Get him cleaned up and have a healer come take a look at him. We will send him on his way once we start our journey. We must keep him unconscious until then," Anthony said as he walked out of the cell.

"Where are you off to, son?"

"I need to check on Viviana and tell Lord Bion about what we have learned. Do you think you can handle it from here?" Anthony looked at his father.

"Go, I can take care of this mess," Marcus said. Anthony bowed to his father and left. The war was coming soon, and he knew his father would take care of the Manor. He just hoped they all would make it out alive.

Anthony found Lord Bion at Viviana's bedside. He cleared his throat to signal his presence and saw his uncle motion to the room across the hall.

"How is she?" Anthony asked as Lord Bion closed the door.

"She is tough," he said as he sat in the chair by the fireplace and motioned for Anthony to join him.

"Yes, she is…" Anthony's voice trailed off.

"Rest your worries. Your mother assures me she has pulled through the worst of it. So, what news do you bring me?"

"It seems the king is having nightmares. The queen is interpreting them and blaming Viviana for them, which is why the king sent the guard. I think the queen is on to us. She may have heard of Vi's abilities…" he stopped speaking as he heard a knock at the door.

"Enter," Lord Bion said.

Euclid stepped in, looking quite worried.

"We came down here just as soon as we could. Adilynn is with Viviana now. I am so sorry…"

Lord Bion stood and placed his hand on Euclid's shoulder. "Come now, she is going to be fine. This is not your doing."

"But the wedding…"

"It is not the wedding's fault, either." He waved his hand dismissively. "This matter is being dealt with as we speak, and we have nothing to fear." Lord Bion smiled, trying to reassure Euclid.

73

Another knock came.

"Enter," Lord Bion said.

Mathilda appeared with a tray of food.

"This should keep your stomach in check until dinner is ready. Viviana is recovering nicely, so you men can go about your tasks and stop wasting your time in the healing house. Got it?" She looked directly at Lord Bion and Anthony.

"Yes, madam." Lord Bion smiled at his sister-in-law and bowed his head as a sign of gratitude and respect.

"So, shall we go and finalize the travel arrangements, then?" Euclid asked as they left the room and made their way to the library.

Chapter 9

The morning came and went as the preparations for the wedding continued. The smell of fresh herbs and roasting meats lingered in the air as the halls filled with more and more guests. After the attack on Viviana, everyone in the Manor was on high alert. Guards were checking everyone coming in and out of town.

There were only two days before the wedding and still Viviana slept in the healing house. They posted guards at every entrance, and two were at the healing house at all times. Mathilda checked on her several times during the day and was amazed that the wound was already healed. She saw the color return to her cheeks, and by the evening Viviana was awake.

"Auntie, where am I?" she asked as she tried to focus her eyes.

"My dear child, you are awake." Mathilda kissed her forehead sweetly as tears rolled down her cheek. "You are in the healing house. Do you remember anything?"

"I… I was stabbed…" She felt her stomach and felt no pain. In fact, she felt as if nothing happened. She looked around the room and saw the pitcher of water on the table.

"I will let your father know you are awake."

"No," she got out of bed. "I need to go see him. May I have a robe?" Her loose hair swayed as she moved to the table to get a drink of water.

"But child, you were attacked just two days ago, and you should not be up walking." Mathilda tried to get her back in bed.

"Auntie, thank you for your concern, but I am capable of walking." She would not be babied.

"I will escort you then," her aunt said with determination in her voice.

"I would like that," she said and hugged her warmly.

They made their way to the war room, where they found Lord Bion in his chair with his head propped up by his hand. He seemed to be sleeping. Viviana turned to her aunt.

"Thank you, Auntie. I would like to speak to father alone if I may."

Mathilda searched her niece's eyes before finally conceding with a nod. Viviana gave her another hug and Mathilda left. Turning back to the war room, Viviana knocked softly, rousing her father.

"Viviana, what are you doing up? You should still be in bed." He got up and tried to put his arms around her, but she pushed him away.

"I am fine, father. Remember my witch abilities that allow me to heal from just about anything?" she said with such malice that her father balked.

"Why are you in such a mood, my child?" He moved towards her again.

"How about the fact that the queen tried to have me killed? How did that bastard get in here?"

"Anthony asked the assassin. He stole some clothes from a merchant and posed as the wine delivery man. Mathilda checked the wine over and paid him, but she watched him walk out the back door and leave. At least that's what she thought. With the wedding…"

"I know. It's a madhouse with all the new people and caravans of things coming into the Manor. So, was I the target because I am your daughter?"

He nodded.

"Then there is no time to wait for the wedding. We should leave now." She tried to leave the room, but her father placed his hand on her shoulder.

"No, you must be at the wedding. It is not safe to travel at night, and I have arranged for a companion for your travels. I think you will like him. He will meet us on the road."

"Who?" She cocked her head to the side. "Who can keep us safe on the road when creatures and knights are hunting us?"

"I only know of one… person."

"Remus? You really asked him to come? Is it safe for him to come? I would not want him to get hurt because of me."

"It's his way of paying back Mathilda by protecting her children and mine when we cannot."

"Thank you for asking him. I will feel safer with him by my side," she said.

"And Anthony?" He raised one eyebrow.

"I don't know if I am safe around him or not," she said. "He is not the same as those monsters, but he *is* a knight. I'm still trying to keep my feelings in check."

"Please try to do so on this journey. I know it is a daunting task I ask of you, Vi. But I know you will come to trust and care for Anthony. He will need you as much as you will need him." Her father smiled.

"Need me? How so?" She was curious.

"As a friend and as his healer. Remember, this is a treacherous path you two are traveling. Who knows what dangers are out there and even with Remus around…"? He stopped when he heard a light tap on the door. "Enter."

"Pardon my intrusion, my lord. I wanted to let you know that Sir Marcus needs your assistance." Gordon, a young guard from the dungeon, smiled at seeing Viviana.

She smiled back as she moved past him and out the door. "I am going to my room. See you at dinner, father." She walked away, leaving the men talking about the prisoner. Hearing anymore about her attacker would make her angry and that was an emotion she could not afford to feel. Besides, she still had more packing to do.

Once Viviana finished gathering her things, she looked at her room and saw how empty it was. The drawing of her mother sat by her bed still, and she went to retrieve it. Those beautiful almond-shaped eyes and flowing hair made her look like the Calestius women in the history books. Viviana ached to be held in her arms again. Nine years had flown by, but she could still hear her laughter and feel her embrace.

Tears rolled down her cheeks as she sat on her bed. She let the sadness wash over her while she held her mother's picture. She hoped she'd be able to share in the joy of Adilynn's last festival.

"Alright, missy!" Adilynn's voice pulled her out of her thoughts, startling her. "Mother arranged a Hen Party for me at the tavern with the womenfolk. We shall sing and dance and be merry!" she shouted and pulled Viviana from the bed. "I brought you your dress and your badge of honor." The badge had 'Master's slave' on it. Viviana giggled at the reference to her being the maid of honor, which they always joked was just the bride's slave. She wiped away the rest of her tears and followed her cousin out of the room. It was time to have some fun.

Chapter 10

"It's time to get up and ready for my wedding!" Adilynn yelled at Viviana's protest to get up. Viviana grabbed for the closest object and hurled it at her obnoxious cousin. It missed by several feet.

"Damn it," she mumbled, and looked at her cousin with one eye open.

"It's not my fault you had too much mead last night." Adilynn pulled the covers back and tickled her feet. Viviana kicked at her as she laughed, trying not to get her in the face.

"Stop it," Viviana said and slowly got up from her bed. They made their way to the room filled with the wedding attire and got dressed.

"My word." Viviana smiled as she admired her reflection. The emerald and gold silk dress hugged every curve of her frame. Even though the neckline and loose flowing straps showed too much skin, Viviana was not nervous about it. Her father wouldn't be happy with the choice of style, but Adilynn wanted something exotic, and she was the bride. So, the dresses were made like those in the Calestius' court. The simple hairstyle and flowers made the women look as if they walked out of a fairytale book. This event would be the most talked about wedding for years to come.

"What do you think, cousin?" She turned to see Adilynn in her ivory silk dress embroidered with emerald and gold flowers in silk on the bodice. The cascading pattern continued all the way down the train of the gown.

"You are radiant," Viviana said, and knew that every eye would be on the blushing bride-to-be.

As they were finishing, Mathilda knocked on the door and startled the two girls. She gave the girls a sad smile. Adilynn started to tear a little and ran to her mother. They hugged each other, needing no words at the moment.

"My sweetest little girl," Mathilda started, "you have grown into such a beautiful young lady. It makes your father and me so proud that you have found love."

"It helps that his family is wealthy," Viviana remarked with a note of bitterness in her voice, drawing the scowls of both ladies before her.

"Now you of all people know I would marry him if he was a pauper," Adilynn said. "Love is the only thing to marry for."

"Shame on you, Viviana! How could you speak such nonsense to your cousin on her wedding day? This is a day to celebrate love and family and new beginnings."

"She was just being Viviana. She knows how amazing Euclid is for me. She will find her own soon enough," Adilynn said, giving her cousin a smile.

Viviana cringed. Mathilda was right; it was not fair for Viviana to be so hateful on such a day.

"I am sorry," Viviana offered, her eyes to the floor.

"Be strong, my child. The journey you face holds your destiny. You will know soon how you fit in this world." Mathilda hugged her fiercely. This simple act made Viviana miss her mother dearly at that very moment, but she repressed her feelings for later. She had no time to pity her own situation. She hoped with every piece of her soul that her aunt was right.

Adilynn took her downstairs. They needed breakfast before the ceremony, so they didn't faint before dinner. As they entered the dining room, they found a sight to behold. It looked like a battlefield depicted in their history books at school, except their bodies were covered in wine and mead, not blood. Bottles were scattered everywhere, and food was smashed into the floor. A tapestry of some sort hung from the chandelier, but they had no idea where it came from, or how anyone got it up there. Anthony and Euclid were nowhere to be found in the mass of bodies, and the girls hoped that meant they were preparing for the day. The mess, however, was going to take hours to clean. The girls knew Mathilda was going to have a fit, so they escaped before she came downstairs. They found a place to eat and enjoy what little of time they had left together in their home.

"I am going to miss this place." Adilynn looked around her.

"I am going to miss Auntie's cooking. And you, cousin." Viviana placed her head on her cousin's shoulder, trying not to cry.

"No moping now. This is my wedding day!" She tried to sound happy, but her voice gave her true feelings away.

"Adilynn! You're supposed to be at the church now. What is wrong with you?" Anthony looked at them curiously.

Their eyes went to him, then to each other. "I'm just… a little emotional," she said. Viviana couldn't speak.

"You are the one who said yes!"

"I just can't believe it is happening so fast after such a brief engagement."

"Well, sister, it's time to leave the nest and start your own family with the 'man of your dreams', as you constantly remind us," he said.

A smile formed on Adilynn's face. "You're right… he's the man of my dreams!"

Viviana helped her up. "Let's go. There's a wedding waiting for you."

Adilynn beamed and nodded, hurrying out the door. The wedding was in just a matter of moments, and then they would be on the road, heading toward an unknown future together. Viviana didn't know how she was going to do it, but she knew she must go.

They walked silently to the church. Once they arrived, they waited in the hallway. Marcus would come for them in just minutes, and Viviana knew this was the time to give Adilynn her gift.

"We are going to be separated by distance, but you will always have a piece of me, and I will have a piece of you, cousin." She opened a box containing a necklace in two pieces. It was engraved with the word 'sisters.'

"I can't…" Adilynn choked on her tears.

"No words, sister. We are not bound by blood, but by love. No matter what happens when we part ways, I will do all it takes to keep you and your new family safe. I expect to be an aunt soon." They both smiled. "Also, the vial I gave you is the potion that helped save Anthony. You use it on yourself or Euclid if the need arises. Be safe." She gave her cousin a bear hug. They took a deep breath as they both heard the music play.

Here we go. Viviana motioned for the door to open and she walked out to see all the family and friends standing with their hands over their hearts. Their smiles beamed with love and happiness.

As she gracefully glided down the aisle, she focused on breathing. The groom was standing at the front facing the wall, with his cloak over his head. She walked up to the front and rang the bell sitting on the table. The music stopped and everyone sat down. Her voice crackled as she sang.

"Prepare yourself. Prepare yourself. The time for love is here. Raise your eyes. Raise your eyes. The bride now comes; the bride is near." She repeated these lines until Adilynn reached the front of the hall.

"The bride is here. She waits for her groom," Viviana said, and all eyes turned to Euclid. His shoulders relaxed, and he removed his hood, still not looking at his bride.

"I dare not look her way, for her beauty and grace will blind me."

"My love," Adilynn said, "you should not fear. Your faithfulness and kindness will protect your sight. Please gaze upon me, so we may unite as one on this day."

Euclid turned and smiled. Everyone cheered as they held hands and recited their marriage pledge to each other. Then their mothers bound their hands with a silken rope while reciting a poem written by Euclid's mother.

"Let your hearts be bright,
Your love remains ever strong.
Be one in your thoughts.
Have patience each day.

Grow in the garden of love,
And always hold hands."

"Now you may kiss the bride," the minister said as the room filled with applause. The happy couple bowed to their guests, who bowed back to them as a sign of respect and love. The ceremony ended as the sun rose high in the sky, and the reception began with a meal fit for a king and queen. For the next four hours, they filled the Manor with laughter, music, and celebration. Too soon it was over and time for their departure. Mathilda guided the newlyweds to their cottage on wheels, called a tabergo. This would provide a few comforts of home while traveling, a bed, a stove, and storage for their clothing.

"Be safe, my son and daughter! I will see you in three moons if the weather is favorable." Mathilda hugged them both, while desperately trying not to cry again.

"I will miss you so much, mother!" Adilynn held back her tears as well.

"Come along," Euclid said, "we must prepare to leave soon. Thank you Math—I mean mother. We could not have asked for a better wedding." Euclid hugged Mathilda and then swooped his bride into his arms. With a smile, he carried her into their 'home' for the journey.

"Mother, it is time." Anthony came up to her and kissed his mother sweetly on the cheek.

"I know. You look so much like your father. I just wish I knew you were going to return to me." A single tear rolled down her cheek.

"I will return, and this land will be free of that wretched king and queen when I do. Just keep the Manor from falling apart while we are away." He wiped the tears away. His mother hugged him tightly and then looked around.

"Where did Viviana go? I need to give her something."

"I'm not sure. Let's go look for her together," Anthony said as he took his mother's arm and guided her back to the Manor.

Chapter 11

"Daughter, are you prepared for your travels? We must depart within the hour."

"We? Are you coming?"

"Just until the end of my land. I need to speak to Lord Barabous about guarding the caravan to Euclid's father's lands. They are very close to the border between Dragoonus and Calestius. It is there you will cross and travel with some palace guards to the Sun Shrine. Queen Loviana will be waiting for you." He grinned at the smile on Viviana's face. She didn't want to say goodbye just yet, so the news of her father coming along was comforting.

"Thank you, father!" She threw herself into his warm embrace. "I am excited you will ensure our safety along the way." She laughed at her sarcasm. She knew he was hesitant to let her go just yet, as well. He picked her up like a rag doll and hugged her fiercely. She knew she sensed her fear about the impending journey and wanted to ease her mind.

"I am finished and quite exhausted." She sat on her bed and fixed her hair. "I may just head down to our tabergo and take a nap."

"You mean yours. I will sleep with the guards just like a good leader should. I don't think you need your grizzly father sleeping next to you to protect you," he said while picking up her trunk. "You should go and make sure Moonkiss is ready to travel."

"Will do," she said and kissed him on the cheek. She headed out the door and down to the stables.

Viviana's thoughts wandered as she walked towards the stall of her horse. Her eyes welled at the idea of being far away from home and not knowing when she would be back. A soft neigh made her focus on the tall black figure in front of her. *My Moonkiss.* She stroked his neck as she checked the straps on his bridle. He was coming with them; one piece of home would be with her always. She stroked the stallion's mane when a memory interrupted her peace, and a flash of anger returned.

"Viviana?" Anthony's voice was barely louder than a whisper and she thought for a moment she was dreaming, but then she felt his hand touch her shoulder.

"Anthony, I was just…" She realized how she must look at him and tried to wipe her face clean.

"Are you alright?" He moved closer to her.

"I'm fine," she said as she started brushing Moonkiss' mane. "What do you need?"

"Uncle said you would be here. I'm afraid it's time to go," he said. She nodded and walked away from her stallion, but stumbled and fell into the hay.

"Are you alright this time?" Anthony chuckled as he helped her to her feet.

"I wish you wouldn't be such a knight, trying to help me all the time," she said as she brushed hay from her dress. She realized he still was holding her hand. She looked at him and gingerly removed her hand from his.

"Well, if you were not such a damsel in distress, then I would not have to save you - or at least try to save you - all the time," he said, walking with her to the caravan. She couldn't say anything to him, but secretly she wanted to be saved.

As they walked, they could see everyone gathered close to the gate. The caravan was ready. Adilynn and Euclid had their own tabergo, and she had one for herself. A dozen of her father's best guards were going with them for protection. Since the attack on her life, all her father thought about was the safety of everyone around her. They would take every precaution while traveling to Euclid's estate, which was just a day's ride from the border of Calestius.

"Mount up," her father's booming voice stirred the men into action and the caravan started the five-day journey. The married couple stayed secluded in their traveling honeymoon suite for the first leg of the trip. Viviana read, wrote, and practiced knitting during the day, peeking her head out from time to time to see the countryside and talk to her father. Anthony remained quiet and seemed preoccupied with keeping an eye out for danger.

On the third day of traveling, they stopped at an inn to rest and gather supplies. Viviana was excited for a bath and a bed that didn't rock with the movement of the road. She loved her little home on wheels and her bed, but the ride was hard on her and she already felt homesick. Trying to forget about everything, she slipped into the bubble-filled bathtub and drifted into slumber. Then she heard a knock.

"Who is it?"

"It's Adilynn. Can I come in?" The door opened as she asked the question. At least she knocked first. Most of the time she would just come in whenever, since they were like sisters.

"Do you need the tub?" Viviana started to get up from the water.

"Oh, I will once you are finished. I just wanted to come see how you were holding up so far. I know you must be miserable in the tabergo by yourself."

"I am quite content, even though some company like yours would be nice." She winked at Adilynn, and her cousin blushed. "So, how is Euclid in bed?" She sat on a stool and sighed a very content sigh as Viviana stood from the bath and dried off.

"Oh Vi, it is amazing. He is sweet and gentle." She giggled. "It's quite exciting. It is something like chocolate or sweet honey bread, yummy and satisfying for a while. However, if you are with someone who really cares and deeply loves you, you want it all the time. I am quite sore though. I have used muscles that I never knew I had." They both laughed and Viviana reached for more warm water to put in her cousin's bath.

"Well, here you are. Will I see you downstairs for supper or will you be too busy to eat?" Viviana snickered.

"We will be down to dine with everyone else," she said and stuck her tongue out at Viviana as a wet washcloth flew by her head. Viviana ran out the door to her room, which was steps away from the bathroom.

"Anthony, it's not nice to scare me like that." She took a breath after making a face at him.

"Oh, sorry," he mumbled as he averted his eyes. Her thick robe covered her from neck to ankles, yet this still too under dressed for mixed company. She realized

90

she was making him uncomfortable, but it did not embarrass her at all.

"Do not be sorry. I am completely covered, and I am showing much less than most of my wardrobe. Is it so horrid for me to be in a robe?" she asked him rhetorically. He was too busy looking away from her, at least that's what she thought.

"Because a man's mind will think about a woman in such a state of dress. These impure thoughts make men impulsive. Do you understand how easy it would be to subdue you and take advantage of you?" he said, looking deeply into her eyes. They smoldered with something that made Viviana silently gasp and blush a deep crimson color. She recovered quickly and grinned like a drunken fool.

"Well, I think we both know what happens to those who try to subdue me, and I am unwilling," she said, and chuckled.

"True, but what happened at the Manor? You cannot be so flippant about your safety!" His voice and face told her he was angry. She could tell that she had struck a nerve, which made her mad he thought she was not aware of what was at stake. Her anger flared, and she moved him out of the way of her door.

"Yes, father! Oh wait, you are not my father, and I am not a child. I understand my role more than you can imagine. I will do as I please without you!" She slammed the door in his face and let the anger linger. It was easier to be mad at him than to accept he was right. The anger faded, but something else took its place. A flash of Anthony's eyes made her lightheaded. She had strange feelings about her cousin. He made her feel angry and frustrated, but most of the time, she felt safe and protected around him.

"Snap out of it, stupid!" she whispered to herself. It was useless to long for a hero to pick her up and save her from life, especially if that hero was Anthony. He was family and nothing romantic could exist between them. He was a knight and her cousin, even if not by blood, she could never cross that line.

Settling down in her room, she changed for supper. Her wardrobe for the trip was all modest pieces, like the long green tunic with brown pants she grabbed from her travel bag. She also wore a corset made from the hummingbird pattern tapestry that had hung in the halls of her Manor. All her beautiful dresses were packed away.

Sighing, Viviana looked through her jewelry box and saw a small teardrop shaped sapphire necklace. It was one of the first pieces of jewelry her mother had ever given her. Putting it on, she tried to forget about Anthony. At dinner, she hoped to get to chat some with her father about the next leg of the journey.

As she made her way down the stairs, she noticed the small inn had four tables with slightly wobbly chairs. The fire lit the drab little room as warm chatter filled the air. She saw Euclid and Anthony together, and Euclid was quite red and intoxicated by the ale everyone kept buying him. Anthony said something that made the men chuckle around him, and Euclid looked embarrassed.

Viviana made her way to the group to find out what exactly they were talking about when a sudden outcry from the door stopped her in her tracks. A cloaked figure stumbled in, carrying what appeared to be a young woman. Her hair and clothes were splattered with blood as her lifeless arms dangled in the air.

"HELP! Please, help her. I don't know what happened. Oh, God, someone save her... I need a healer." The man's voice trembled as he collapsed to the ground.

Chapter 12

"Dau…" Viviana rushed to the couple, crumpled on the floor. Her father gently picked up the woman and placed her on the floor. The man weakly held onto the woman's hand even though the men tried to help him off the ground.

"No, I must stay with her. Love, my love," he said as he wept.

"I need more light, some warm water and towels," she ordered the men as she tried to examine the wound without causing more damage. They brought lanterns to her, and the barkeeper brought the supplies. She saw the wounds, and they were not as deep as she thought. Viviana started the healing process. The pain she felt with healing Anthony came back, but not as intense. The woman's pale body stirred as the gash on her head disappeared and her broken leg mended. It was wonderful to use her powers without becoming ill herself, but it scared her too. Viviana realized she could not only heal this woman in a short amount of time, but her pain was gone.

"Men, take the woman up to my chambers. I need to see to this gentleman now." She took the man's hand in hers and examined it. He had several defensive cuts on his hands and a gash on his cheek.

"It is a good thing you made it here with all these cuts and with such a badly injured wife," she said and saw the man smile. She had noticed the rings on their fingers as they held hands.

"Yes, it was. I am forever grateful for your help. I am Cornelius, and the woman you saved is Aurora. Some thieves and a strange-looking creature attacked us saved us. He brought us here after promising to bring back our tabergo," he said as he rubbed his newly healed hands.

"Ah, I thought I smelled Remus on you. He is a wonderful friend of mine and is also my protector. But what are you out in the dark traveling in such a dangerous part of Dragoonus?" she asked.

"We are on our honeymoon. We met working in the palace, and I have never met her family, so we thought we would go to Calestius. I want to start a new life there with my wife," he said with hesitation, which Viviana could understand.

"Well, you are safe here." She smiled.

"Thank you, miss. You are such an amazing healer. No one in the palace could match your abilities. What is your name?" Everyone in the room went silent. The question hung in the air, and then Anthony spoke.

"Well, since you are lying to us, maybe we should just give you the same bullshit back, bastard!" The hate in his voice made Viviana quickly move away from the stranger and over to her father.

"You know this man?" Lord Bion said, sounding very perplexed.

"Anthony. I should have known our paths would cross again. I didn't quite expect it to be in such a fashion. I was hoping you would have gotten over the whole thing between you and Aurora, but it sounds like you are still a little bitter about it," the stranger said smugly.

"This is Prince Marius Cornelius, the heir to the mad king's throne." Anthony unsheathed his sword.

"What?" Viviana voiced what everyone else was thinking.

"Well, that's not very nice of you to say about my father. It is true, but still it hurts. I am his son, after all, but my pathetic mother has made him mad. I hope you all are not on that sadistic woman's side." The eyes in the room told him how they all felt about the royal family. "I am going to take that as a no. Good. I am with you and the resistance." He sat down as no one said a word. The tension between Anthony and the prince vibrated the room. No one wanted to set off any sparks and set a fire between the two men.

"My, my, Anthony. I am not unhappy to see you, but please be nice to my husband." The honeydew sweetness in the woman's voice made everyone turn to the stairs. Aurora was awake and looking quite healthy.

"My love, what are you doing up? You should be resting." Cornelius took her hand and kissed it sweetly.

"I am fine, my dear. How many times do I have to tell you not to taunt Anthony for any reason? You should know better," she said as she glided across the room, passing Anthony. He stiffened and moved away as if she hurt him.

Viviana saw his reaction and was curious. *What exactly happened between those two? Were they together at some point?* She knew just who to go ask about it.

"I am glad to see you are up, Aurora. My name is Vi." She smiled sweetly at the woman standing there in her dress.

"The woman upstairs said I could wear this. Thank you." Aurora bowed to Viviana. "We are forever in your debt. I do not know what would have come of me without your swift actions."

"It is just a part of my… gift. Now if you will excuse me, I am a little tired myself." She moved to the stairs and made her way to her room. Feeling everyone's eyes on her, she closed the door and sighed. She wanted to go see Remus, but there were too many people around, and she did not want Anthony following her.

As she waited, she wondered about Aurora and Anthony. *When did they meet? How long ago was it? Did he still have feelings for her?* The thought of him in love with someone stirred that feeling again inside her, of anger and frustration. Or was it something else? She was unsure of this emotion, but whatever it was, it made her quite uneasy. Hopefully, knowing more from Remus would help curb her curiosity. For now, anyway.

She fell asleep and woke with a tray of food sitting on her table. The healing must have hit her more than she realized as she saw the twinkling stars in the sky.

After eating swiftly, she grabbed her cloak and opened her door to see Anthony. His arms were folded across his chest and his head up, but she could see his eyes were closed. Hoping he was deep asleep, she tiptoed out of her room and to the top of the stairs.

"And where are you going at this time of night?" His deep, husky voice sounded tired. *So much for going alone.*

"I wanted to see how Remus is doing. This is the time of night I would normally visit him in the woods. Besides, I can't sleep." She was being honest, at least about where she was going.

"Then I will come with you." He got up from his chair.

"Fine, but keep your distance. I wish to speak with him alone." She folded her arms and stood there, waiting for his response.

"About?"

"Private matters."

"So, he is your confidant?" He cocked his head and smiled.

"One of them." She was not smiling. He was annoying her with his questions.

"How about me?" The question left her stunned. *Him? Tell him my secrets?*

"You are my cousin and my sworn protector, but that doesn't mean I can trust you with everything yet." She gave him a half smile and turned to go down the stairs. Missing the step, she fell.

"Got you." His voice was close to her ear and his arms were wrapped around her waist.

"You can let go now," she said meekly as the feeling of butterflies danced around in her stomach. *Please not now!*

"I will let go when you are safely at the bottom of the stairs." He scooped her up and carried her down the staircase. She held onto his neck but couldn't look at him. The feeling of his arm muscles twitching made her face flush. *Hopefully, he can't see me blushing.*

97

He sat her down, and she pushed away from him. Her heart was racing, and the butterflies flew faster. This feeling was making her scared and then angry. Not at him, but at herself.

"Are you alright, Vi?" he asked with concern in his voice.

"Yes, I'm fine. Probably still just a bit weak from today." She curled a loose strand of her hair around her finger. She stopped when she saw him staring at her. *Those green eyes, again.*

"Maybe you should go back to bed," he said and moved closer to her.

"That sounds like a good idea, actually." She moved back to the staircase.

"Goodnight then," he said.

"Goodnight," she said and made her way back up the stairs to her room. As she closed the door, she heard his footsteps and the chair move against the floor. She assumed Anthony would continue his guard duty through the night, hindering her plan for going out. Sighing, she got back into bed and wondered about what tomorrow would bring. *What would they do about Cornelius and Aurora? How would it affect the journey? Could they be trusted?*

These musings would not let her sleep, so she tried to find something else to think about and that's when her mind replayed the first time she saw Anthony. *Those green eyes.* The memory made her smile.

"Stop that," she whispered, scolding herself. *He is my cousin. No matter what, he is my cousin.* Drifting off to sleep, she smiled and let the dreamless darkness take over her.

Chapter 13

Viviana awoke to the sound of a crash from downstairs. She hurried to dress and ran from her room to see Cornelius and Anthony at each other's throats. Her father was trying to separate them without getting hurt in the process.

"What on earth is going on?" she asked loudly as she descended the stairs. Her eyes landed on the three men in the middle of the room. She cocked her head and placed her hands on her hips, just like Aunt Mathilda.

"This damn, wretched fiend implied that my beautiful wife is a liar. I will not stand for such…" Cornelius' face flushed with a crimson hue.

"I think you and Aurora are here just to spy on us." Anthony sat down in a chair. He looked tired.

"I speak the truth. I am a spy from Calestius. The queen sent me to be her ears and eyes. Here is my proof," Aurora said as she held out an amulet. Lord Bion held it up to the firelight and made a grumbling sound. Viviana knew he was not happy about it, but they were telling the truth, at least enough for the moment.

"I believe you," Lord Bion said as he sat down. "Queen Loviana told me about you when you were to wed Anthony." Viviana's eyes grew as Anthony looked away from everyone and stared at the fireplace. She looked at Adilynn and she motioned to her to go outside. They snuck out as Lord Bion continued to speak with the prince and his wife.

"Viviana, what is wrong?"

"Nothing. It's just horrid to think that he was in love with that." She blinked and smiled at Adilynn, trying to hide her feelings. She didn't want to hate this girl, yet she did. It felt right, but so wrong, too. Anthony was off limits to her, so why could she not stop herself from these feelings?

"Well, he tried to hide this from all of us for a very long time. It was not until his last visit that he even admitted that he was engaged. But it was over by that time. She moved on to the prince, and again, her duty. She is a trained spy for Calestius and was raised from a young age for this assignment. I can't imagine being raised as a spy for Dragoonus."

"Like Anthony?" Viviana said aloud. "They trained him to be my protector, but he also had to learn the secrets of the palace for the resistance to have what they needed to survive and fight the monarch. And then there is me, who has a gift that can be used against all the people I love. I do not wish to be a weapon for anyone," she said and turned to her cousin. Adilynn had tears in her eyes and moved swiftly to embrace Viviana.

"You are not a weapon. You are an amazing and beautiful woman who has a gift for healing. We never saw you as a monster, or weapon, or anything like that.

Mathilda trained you as best she could, but you are more powerful than we could have fathomed."

"And that's why I must leave everything I know and love in order to train. I have to become better at controlling my powers so I can use this gift as a healer and a warrior. I will be useful when the war begins," she said to herself, and her cousin smiled.

"You will be mightier than all the king's knights rolled into one!" Adilynn struck a pose that made Viviana laugh so hard it made her sides hurt. Her fear and anxiety always went away around her cousin. She would miss her terribly. "So, do you think uncle will let them travel with us?"

"What?!" Viviana was shocked at the idea. She mulled it over for a moment. "That would be a good idea. He could keep tabs on them and make sure we deliver them over the border, so they don't have a chance to run back to the queen," Viviana said.

"I know Anthony will not be happy with that idea." Adilynn shook her head.

"He will be even more distant and grumpy than normal, but he will see the logic behind it. Besides, we might have to use the prince for leverage at some point." She giggled a little at the thought of Anthony tying up the prince in ropes and throwing him into the back of one of the tabergos.

"Why Vi, you are quite devilish, but that makes sense. I think his mother just might like the heir to be alive, unless she wants him dead?" Adilynn shivered at the thought.

"Depends on if she believes him a victim or a willing participant. That will make all the difference. He could be more trouble than he is worth." Viviana thought out loud about her fears.

101

"Let us go eat, cousin. The next stop won't be until we get to Lord Barabous' land." Both cringed at the fact that they would go another four days without bathing and good cooking.

The trip was much like the one to the University and they never wanted to go through that again. Yet, here they were, and Viviana cursed at herself. She wished she could go back home already. She wished the entire journey was a bad dream she'd wake up from tomorrow.

When they entered the inn, everyone sat together eating their morning meal. They sat down and tried to enjoy their time together. While they talked about the next leg of the trip, her father came over and asked to speak with Viviana alone. Her cousin left and went to sit with Euclid and Anthony.

"Yes, father?" Viviana smiled at her father, and he smiled back.

"I just wanted to let you know we are here for one more day. Cornelius and Aurora need to rest before traveling…"

"Traveling with us?"

"Yes. Do you approve?" he asked.

"Of course. It is a great idea to keep them close, but you do not need my approval."

"I know, but your opinion is important to me." He lovingly put his arm around her shoulders. She looked at his worried eyes. Leaning into him, she placed her head on his chest. Viviana could hear the steady beat of his heart and it helped calm her nerves.

"Thank you, father. I am happy you made that decision. It is good to keep an eye on them, especially since they have seen what I can do with my healing powers. Even if Aurora is a spy for Calestius, I do not trust her or the prince," she whispered as she picked her head up from his chest.

"Well said, my daughter. You are as wise as you are beautiful. I knew all those lessons in the war room would pay off." He smiled.

"Now I am going to see how Moonkiss is doing in the barn. I have a treat for him." She walked towards the door, while keeping her eye on Anthony. He seemed like he was deep in conversation and would not notice her leaving. She walked swiftly to the barn and grabbed her dream journal from her satchel. The last few days, her dreams were so vivid that they scared her and that was one more topic she needed to discuss with Remus. He was a wise man who knew how to listen to her, without trying to fix everything like the others.

Viviana settled down on a bench close to a wishing well and waited for Remus. She had told no one else about her dreams. They were vivid as the forest in front of her and it made her shiver. The small journal she hid in a shirt pocket was filled with all the nightmarish images floating in her mind. They haunted her, but she dared not reveal anything to anyone else, or they might think her mad. She shook the images away and looked into the woods for a sign of her hairy friend.

"Remus!" she yelled at the edge of the forest right by the inn. She thought she saw him go in, but now she felt uneasy. She sensed something or someone was watching her, and she walked back to the inn. As she reached the barn again, she was grabbed from behind. Her scream echoed around her, and men appeared from everywhere at once. Remus was the one who got to her first and ripped the claws from around her. The creature that held her was a strange mix of bird and beast. The face was not human at all, but it was the size of Anthony, and she could see intelligence in its eyes. Remus slammed it to the ground and fought until it stopped moving. The creature was still breathing but lay there unconscious. Viviana stood there in a daze, and it took two of her father's guards to move her.

"Viviana, are you alright?" Her father looked at her arms and face. She only had a few scrapes that had already almost healed. Her head reeled from what had just happened, and she just could not form a coherent sentence. All she did was nod yes and no to his questions. She just watched as Remus rushed the guards to bind the creature with chains and rope. Lord Bion forced Viviana to go to her room with Adilynn. As she walked away, she kept her gaze on the beast that had its claws around her just moments ago. She stopped and refused to leave. Anthony picked her up and headed for the inn.

"How dare you!" She kicked and flared her arms but did not allow her emotions to get the better of her. After all she had done to Anthony before, she could not afford to be truly angry with him.

"Hold still and I will put you down in the inn," he said as they got close to the front of the inn.

"No, I want down now. I have to see what grabbed me. I do not think it meant to harm me." She wiggled enough that he lost control of her and had to put her down before he dropped her.

"Are you mad? It put its claws into your skin. It could have ripped you to shreds." He looked at her like she had lost her mind.

"No, I am quite sane, and it did not mean to leave any marks on me. I moved when Remus attacked it and it did not have time to let go. I could feel it loosening its grip when it happened," she said, running over to the crowd.

She snaked her way through until she was right in front of the creature. It was awake and smiling at her.

"I am so sorry, little one. I did not mean to come here like this and cause you any pain." The voice of an old and wise elder came from the beast. "I am Oryn, a servant to the Queen of Calestius. She wanted me to bring you a message, but I could not change quickly enough before we met. I have become slow in my old age." He chuckled to himself. "It took me quite by surprise to smell the scent of a man I assumed died long ago, Theron." His dark orange eyes looked deeply into Remus'.

"Master Oryn!" Remus removed the bonds before anyone could protest.

"Remus, that creature attacked…"

"Father, he didn't hurt me on purpose. The marks were due to him trying to let me go when Remus grabbed him. Master Oryn just startled me when he appeared and that is why I screamed."

"Glad you did not turn on him," Anthony said while holding his arm. His comment and smile made Viviana blush. She gave him a dirty look and said nothing. He winked at her and her heart skipped a beat again. She hoped no one saw it. She spun away from him and back to the creature that now stood in front of her as a man. He appeared older than her father and had thin snow-white hair with a beard to match. His eyes were still the orange color that reminded her of a fall sunset. While his eyes were an odd color, it was his hands that caught her by surprise. They were like cat paws, with hair and claws, and he waved at her with a goofy grin on his face. She did not know why, but it made her giggle like a little girl being tickled by her father. It was so very amusing to her.

"So, I see my cat paws still work on young ladies with good hearts," he said with enthusiasm. Everyone else just stood staring at the man. They didn't know quite what to make of him and turned to Lord Bion, who was staring just like the rest of them. He quickly motioned to Master Oryn to come join them in the inn. Master Oryn bowed gracefully and with a flick of his wrist, his paws became those of a man. He then followed the crowd into the small and now very loud inn.

"So, what news do you bring to us?" Lord Bion asked as he gave Master Oryn a drink.

"The Queen of Dragoonus' guards are patrolling the roads from here to the border. She is looking for something, or perchance, someone?"

"Probably her son, Master Oryn," Viviana said as she joined the men at the table.

"This is what my sources are telling me, yes, little one. However, that gives them just cause to search everyone going across the border. We are hoping to keep our precious treasure," he winked at Viviana, "from being found out and taken before she reaches her destination."

She knew he was right. Their journey now was more dangerous than before. Lord Bion took the news hard. He'd hope that the journey would stay safe at least through Dragoonus, but it looked like they would have to be twice as cautious. They had to regroup before traveling and retool the plan.

"The road to your friend's keeps that you are traveling to seems to be safe for now. As I traveled this way, I made sure of it." He winked at Viviana. "However, I am not sure about the road between Mr. Greenfield's land and the border. Pardon me, I should say Lord Fangstrom's since he has the old lord's land." He looked at Euclid and bowed his head slightly. Euclid did not like the fact that everyone knew his newly acquired land came from the old lord, who willed it to him after Euclid saved his life.

"Well, that road is one of the main ones in that area to the border, and I would not be surprised if they bulked up the guards there. I am glad we have all the documents we need," Lord Bion said, and then frowned. "By Dragoonus' beard. What about the prince?"

"Do not worry about me and my wife. We have prepared for anything." The prince's voice made everyone turn to the door, except for Master Oryn.

"Ah, so the prince has shown up. I do not even need to turn and see you. It is your tone of voice," Master Oryn said, and turned. "I can also tell by the way you carry yourself and that face. Anyone close to the court will know you instantly. I think work must be done so that you can pass as a simple peasant of the kingdom, or they will find you out. I am surprised you even got this far without help." He eyed the prince and saw the young man's face turn bright red.

"How dare you speak to me that way, old man!" The heat from the fire drew to the prince like a moth to a flame. Viviana spotted the signs of trouble and knew she had to calm him down before he did any damage.

"Your highness needs to be in better control, or you will cause harm to those around you. Think of your wife who is upstairs now. You do not want to save her from what you have caused." Her voice and the mention of Aurora forced him to realize what he was doing. He hastened to the stairs and went to his room, closing the door with force behind him.

"Viviana, was that what I think it was?" Anthony said with a note of fear in his voice. He knew what this meant to the traveling party if the prince had the same abilities as Viviana.

"I guess I am not the only one to watch out for. I hope for all of us that this is not his level of control. It would be highly dangerous for us all to travel with those two," Viviana said, speaking what was on her father's mind.

"However, they know about us, and it would be problematic if they were found. So, we are stuck between a rock and a mountain," Anthony said, and looked at Viviana.

"Not necessarily. It just means I have to get close to him and see how much help he needs. If I can help him keep himself in check until we get to the border..." Viviana trailed off and looked at Lord Bion.

"You need to be careful of that bastard. Even if he is married, he will try to take advantage of you," Anthony said through his teeth.

"Anthony, I believe that Vi's idea will work for us. Just keep an eye out for her when she is with the prince. Viviana, give out as little information about yourself as possible. I don't want them to know much more than they do. You are my daughter and a healer going to the Sun Shrine for training."

"Wouldn't they know I am the one his mother is after?" Viviana got nervous about that.

"No, from their story, they left far before that started. I want to keep that as quiet as possible from them," Lord Bion said as he hugged her.

"I will try to remember that when I talk to him at dinner."

"I would suggest we leave now. The news from Master Oryn makes me leery of staying in one place too long," Euclid stated as he took a bag out to the tabergo.

"You are right. We will prepare to move out immediately. You are more than welcome to join us," Lord Bion said to Master Oryn. He bowed gracefully.

"I shall. The queen asked me to help as much as possible. Besides, I have been dying to get to know Viviana. She's the talk of the Sun Shrine. They heard of her coming with those abilities and are quite impressed."

Viviana blushed a deep crimson red. It embarrassed her to know people she had never met talked about her. As she thought about her newfound fame, the men prepared the horses and tabergos for travel. Viviana noticed the addition of the prince and his wife's small carriage to the caravan despite the fear of being found with him. She was very curious to get to know him and his abilities, since she had never met another person with the same power as her own.

Viviana settled down on her bed and gathered her journal. She chronicled the journey and all the events that happened, because she felt all of this would be important to remember. She knew her story would not make sense to others without all the details. As she picked up her pencil, she thought about the prince and his situation. Her perception of him had changed,, and she believed their story more than ever. He was a powerful tool, which his mother could use to do her bidding if he was captured. She was curious why he didn't heal his wife, however, when they came to the inn. She decided that would be her question the next time they talked.

She continued to write her story when the caravan stopped. She popped her head out to see Remus lifting an oak tree out of the road. She could see the intensity in Anthony and her father's face and knew they were anxious. They were waiting for an ambush, Viviana concluded. She had heard that thieves set traps and then jump out from the trees to steal what they could from the unsuspecting travelers. They were still on her father's land, but the forest was filled with things he knew little about. He did not have the resources to protect everyone and everything on the edge of his land. He left that up to the townspeople who lived around these areas.

"The road is clear. Proceed carefully," Remus said as he led the caravan.

"Is something out there?" Viviana asked her father, who rode next to her window.

"There may be, but Remus mentioned nothing. I think he just wants us all to stay alert. You should go back to your studies. Are you ready for the exam?" Viviana cringed at the mention of it.

"I have prepared as much as I can. I don't know exactly what's on the test. I am quite familiar with many subjects from the University, but I am unsure how that will help me."

"I am sure you will do well, but you can never be too prepared," he said, and winked. That was her father's favorite motto, and he would never let her forget it. She rolled her eyes at him and closed her window.

She looked at the books scattered on the floor and sighed. Nothing was further from her mind since she was thinking about her birthday. It was in a few days, and she was not happy being on the road. Viviana went to her bed and lay down. The sun descended, passed the trees, and decorated the forest with hues of orange, purple, and red. The call for the caravan to halt came from Lord Bion. When they stopped, Viviana's stomach growled, and she longed for her aunt's cooking. She was thinking about her aunt when she heard a tap on her window.

"Yes?" She threw open the window.

"How are you doing?" Anthony asked sweetly.

"Bored," she said as she saw his face. His eyes were bright and focused. They made her blush, and he could see it in the last bit of sunlight left.

"What are you blushing about?"

"Women blush about many things," she said as she tried to hide her face.

"What are you blushing about?" he asked her again.

"You will laugh if I tell you," she said sheepishly.

"No, I won't, unless it's silly," he said, goading her on.

"Then I will never tell you," she said and stuck her tongue out at him. He moved closer to the window and looked deeply into her eyes. Her cheeks deepened in color, and he gave her an evil grin. His look made her mad at him and she slammed the window in his face. She heard him mumble something, and she flung the window open again.

"What?" she asked in a sharp tone. This time, he blushed and looked flustered.

"Nothing. I didn't say anything." He moved away from the window.

"You did too," she said as she tried to keep him flustered.

"I just said you had a funny way of blushing. You should be careful not to do that around other men, or they might think you are smitten with them." He tried not to say this too loud. Her face became warm, and she shut the window again. She didn't want him hearing her cursing.

What the hell did that mean? Did HE think I was smitten with HIM?

No, he was her cousin. He must just be teasing her.

Viviana tried to calm her mind, but then she realized she would not be able to get rid of him once they reached the Sun Shrine. He wouldn't leave her side for the world,

111

even if it meant his life. He was a handsome and amazing man who she could never be with. No matter how much she wanted to let herself love him, their paths would never allow it.

Viviana's heart ached thinking about never being able to love anyone in such a way. She dreamed of her mystery man who would sweep her from her dull life at the Manor. She enjoyed indulging in this fantasy. Then Anthony came into her life, and she was taken aback by all the feelings and thoughts he stirred inside her. Not only was he ruggedly handsome, but he was also kind, caring, sweet, and fearless. He reminded her of her father. However, he was still her cousin by law and that was a good reason to fight these taboo feelings she had for him.

She sighed and looked toward the window. Viviana wondered if he was close to her and let out a low growl. She could not talk to herself out loud without him possibly hearing her. She missed the privacy of her room and the woods. It was very frustrating to be trapped with her thoughts and feelings. Her heart sank, and she felt homesick again. She blew out her light and chased sleep until dawn.

Chapter 14

As she dozed, she heard a knock on her door. She stumbled and cursed at herself as she tried to wake up. The door swung open to reveal her impatient cousin, Adilynn.

"Hi, Vi. I just wanted to tell you that dinner is ready, and your father requests your presence," she said cheerfully, and Viviana was not happy about it.

"What does he want? I was sleeping quite nicely, and I am not dressed to be out of my tabergo!" she whined.

"He just wants you to come to dinner. He doesn't want his little girl starving," she chuckled at Viviana, who just rolled her eyes.

"Fine, but I have a headache and do not want to be up all night," Viviana grumbled. She had a suspicion her father was up to something. The ladies headed over to the fire and she saw several packages by Lord Bion.

"My darling daughter! You are to turn twenty-one in a foreign land, and I wanted to celebrate with you before we parted." He was so proud, yet so sad. She would do whatever it took to make him happy before they separated.

He gave her a big bear hug and sat her down on his lap like he did when she was little. "I am so proud of you. Since you were a babe, I just wanted you to be happy and do good with your life. You are going to take on so much without me by your side, but my love will go with you. You are the most precious gift your mother could have given me." He tried to hide the sorrow in his voice.

"I , father. She would be so happy to see me become an outstanding scholar and supporter of my family." She chose her words carefully with the prince and his wife in the crowd.

"Before we eat, let's open some presents!" He grinned as he handed her a beautiful oak and silver bow with a quiver of arrows.

"Now I have to practice archery again," she said and sighed loudly. Everyone laughed, since she was the best archer in their town. She played with the bow when her father handed her a small box. It was lined with beautiful dark blue material and held a small locket shaped like a rose. When she opened it up, she saw it held a piece of a rose from the garden.

"It's beautiful!" Viviana cried and had her father help her put it on. As he did, he whispered who made it for her. She looked at Anthony, who grinned like a fool at her. She blushed as he bowed his head to her.

"Thank you, cousin. It looks like it's from our garden roses at home, but how?"

"Your father mentioned you planted them with Lady Ambrosiana when you were little. I thought it would be nice if you had something from home with you," he said and looked deeply into her eyes until Remus' vast shadow startled them.

"Here you are, my little troublemaker! I hope this will keep you warm when it gets cold in Calestius. The wind at the tower is very bitter at night." He put the cloak around her, and she felt the fur on the inside.

"It feels soft like you," she said, hugging him with all her might. She was grateful for such a devoted friend. Lord Bion motioned for the men to play some music and the party began.

Anthony watched Viviana and Adilynn dancing around the fire and wanted to join them, but he had to continue his patrol around the camp. With the music, the group was more vulnerable to attack if anyone was out in the woods.

"What are you smiling about?" Remus asked as he looked at the group.

"I'm just enjoying listening to Viviana's singing. She is having fun."

"You look like you are enjoying being around Viviana," Remus said, and smiled. There was something in his voice that made Anthony look away.

"I missed so much while I was gone. I was happy only when I was with Aurora at the palace and now, being around her... I'm happy, but it's quite complicated. Isn't it?" He looked at his old master and sighed.

"Life is complicated, young one. However, if you stay true to your path and use both your head and heart, then I can see a bright future for you. And for Vi." Remus walked with Anthony. "And love. It is a hard task, especially for a heart that is weak and worn from past experiences. Trust me, I know."

"I know, master, but I can't let my emotions get in the way of the journey. Then there is the uncertainty of our relationship. It makes it hard to know how to act around her," he said as his eyes locked onto the fire where

115

he heard Viviana and Cornelius' voices. He watched as they talked. It looked like she had started her mission to find out more information on the prince's powers. While giggling at something he said, she twirled a loose strand of hair. She appeared to be flirting. Remus watched Anthony grab the hilt of his sword with a tight grip and move closer to the couple. They both could hear them talking cordially about the trip, and then Viviana asked more prying questions.

"So why did you become so angry when Master Oryn talked to you?" Viviana used her honey-sweet voice while talking to him. Anthony could tell the prince was very focused on her eyes and lips.

"I simply hate people talking to me like that. He was being quite condescending. But I tend to overreact, and of course, that is one of my many flaws that Aurora likes to point out. She is right, though."

"I noticed your body and even the room became very warm when you reacted. Does this happen every time?"

"Well, as one healer to another, you should know how hard it is to control our 'gift,' if that is what you want to call it. My mother says this 'blessing' has a curse that goes along with it. Our emotions fuel this ability, and it can go either way. Our feelings are also guided by our innate need to protect others or protect ourselves. The curse is to keep us safe, but it destroys the ones we love. It comes from our blood, the Calestius blood. We are related in some way, and I think we both will benefit from going to the Shrine. I hope we can be friends, Viviana." His smile seemed genuine, and she wanted to trust him. Her thoughts switched from him to Anthony as she saw him out of the corner of her eye.

She excused herself and headed towards Anthony. She knew he was just keeping tabs on her for her father, but it still didn't make her happy. Viviana snickered to herself when she thought of having some fun with him. She casually walked over by him, as he seemed to stare off into space.

"So, spying on me again?" she said with a smile. Anthony didn't know quite how to answer the question and just stood there. She moved closer to him and put her hand gently on his shoulder. It made him shiver.

"You are going to play dumb now? I think you don't like seeing me with the prince. Am I right?" He stiffened and glared at her. She was enjoying his reaction and pushed a little further. "So, I shouldn't talk to him? I was just having a simple conversation with a man I am supposed to get close to."

"I know how he treats women, and it's disgusting to watch you flirt with him! Your father said to get information from him, not to become buddies with him," he said through his teeth.

"Well, it's easier to get what you want from men with honey," she said with her back to Anthony.

"And what am I?" he asked and walked away from her. "I guess you don't need anything from me!" he said with such anger in his voice that it startled Viviana. She had pushed a little too much and reeled him back in.

"I need you to protect me, cousin. Besides, I am just teasing you, as our family does to each other. Please don't be mad at me." She pouted and then smiled sweetly. He looked into her eyes and then just walked away from her, leaving her standing there confused. Confusion turned to anger, and she stormed off after him.

"Wait a second, Anthony." She caught up to him and grabbed his forearm.

"What?" he said curtly.

"You left me, and I was just trying to have fun with you, cousin."

"So, I am just a toy for you to play with? You sound like all the other women at court," he grumbled.

"Where did this come from?" she asked.

"Nowhere. Now if you will excuse me, your ladyship." He tried to move his arm away from her, but her grip did not lessen.

"In no such manner, will you leave me like this, Anthony. I was simply teasing you, like I would tease your sister or any other member of my family. What has gotten into you?" She was on the verge of tears. His comments made her furious and hurt at the same time.

"It's just... I have to just sit back and watch you with that man?" he grumbled, but there was no anger in his voice. It was still about her talking with Cornelius.

"I am simply finding out information," she said. She locked eyes with him, and she felt that tingle again. Their relationship would have to stay as cousins, but she still wanted to enjoy his company. She hoped they could truly become friends and have fun times while they were together.

"Well, just be careful with the prince."

"And you of Aurora. She's been eyeing you all night." Viviana moved a strand of hair from Anthony's face. He was a very handsome man who she couldn't have as anything more than her cousin. He walked her back to her tabergo and bid her goodnight.

They still had three days before they all could enjoy a day of rest, good homemade food, and showers. He still had patrol duty as the rest of the camp slept and Viviana's father was waiting for her at the door of her tabergo.

"Goodnight, Viviana," Anthony said and kissed her hand. "You as well, Uncle. I am going back to my patrol." He quickly bowed to Lord Bion and left.

"What might I do for you, father?" She seemed suspicious of his visit.

"Can't a father wish his daughter sweet dreams?"

"Or course, but there is something else."

"Well, I also wanted to stress to you that the journey to the Sun Shrine will be treacherous and I need you to follow Anthony's orders to the letter, just like it was me telling you what to do." He emphasized that point and made Viviana nervous. Then she became defiant.

"Orders? He has no right to order me to do anything. He is not my father or husband or, truthfully, anyone who holds any power over me. I only listen to you because you are a wise leader. He might be my sworn protector, but I am of age in three days, which means by law, I am my own person. I do not have to obey anyone!"

"You are as stubborn and pig-headed as your mother. She always argued with me. She hated the word obey, and I am not surprised it passed down to you. Fine, I want you to listen to him as you would listen to me. His first and foremost charge is to keep you safe. If he tells you to fight, to jump, or to run, please, my darling daughter, listen to him. Do not second-guess him the entire way, but be his counsel. I believe that he trusts you and treasures your opinion. Help him keep you safe!" He engulfed her in a bear hug. She truly was too stubborn for her own good sometimes.

"Alright, father. I promise I will listen to Anthony. I am sure we will be fine," she sighed. "He is smart and well-trained. The journey is dangerous, but with the party traveling together, we will reach our destination." She smiled at him and yawned. He wished her pleasant dreams and let her go to bed. She really hated the word obey. It made her feel like property, even with her own father.

Viviana dressed for bed and before her head hit the pillow, she was swept away into a dark and dreamless sleep.

Chapter 15

Daylight crept over the caravan as the campfires were still smoldering from the party. Remus yawned and looked around the woods. He wanted to make sure Viviana was safe before moving on and went to scout ahead. Remus quickly moved through the wooded area just down from the camp. The birds were singing, and he heard running water close by. He found the rushing river and drank deeply of the cool liquid. He breathed in and froze. He could smell ash and blood in the air.

Sprinting back to the camp, he heard a woman's scream. Remus saw the men engaged in battle with several bandits. He went to help them when he saw Viviana and almost laughed. She was sword fighting one of the men and had him cornered. The anger in her eyes told Remus she was on the verge of setting the man on fire, or worse. He saw the man pulling out a dagger and, without warning, the man was airborne. His scream stopped all the fighting.

"Alright, who's next?" Remus licked his lips and smiled. The bandits all stopped, dropped their swords, and ran. One of the younger ones was not swift enough, and Lord Bion caught him.

"Tie this one up! I want answers!" he growled as he tossed the boy to the guards.

"Answers for what? He is a thief and should be put to death!" Cornelius said from his tabergo.

"Strong words from a coward!" Anthony shouted. "Where were you when all of this happened?"

"Guarding the only thing that matters to me," he said, with his arms around Aurora.

"Well, if that's your excuse... I'm sure Aurora can protect herself." He had a very evil grin on his face. "If I recall, you took down two knights guards at that tavern..." The look she gave him made him stop speaking, but he was still smiling.

"If we are finished, children...?" Master Oryn looked at the bandit and studied him. "He is just a boy. He is only eleven or twelve, and not well educated."

"Boy, we are going to let you go, but I need to know about those men you came here with and what they were here for." Lord Bion took the ropes off the boy, who swallowed hard with fear in his eyes. "What is your name?"

"Marius. My family are farmers in this area," he said meekly.

"Why are you with those men?"

"The land has not been good to us, and I am afraid my family will starve this winter. The men needed a guide to get them here. They promised me enough money to help us buy food." He sounded like he was doing everything he could to hold back tears.

"Are we the only ones they have come after?"

122

"Yes. They said they knew of a large caravan traveling this road that had jewels and money with them. They said you were a lord. I was a fool." Marius hung his head in shame.

"Are more coming?" Viviana gave the boy a cup of water. She was afraid of the answer.

"They said if they failed, more would come. I heard many things while I was with the bandits. I am afraid that they will kill me and my family now that I have told you this." He cried.

"Father?" Viviana looked in his eyes and he knew what she wanted. He sighed and shook his head.

"You shall come with us then Marius and go back to your family after Lord Bion comes back this way." Viviana saw a mix of relief and fear from the boy.

"But my family? How will they know? Will they be hurt for my actions?"

"I will send two of my men to your parents. We will let them know you are in my custody until we come back. They will take enough money to make sure your family is taken care of. Adonius and Bactus report back to Marcus when you are done with the boy's family. I want him to know what is going on with my land out here. Be safe!" He grabbed their arms and shook them once. They were just like Lord Bion's sons, and he was sending them on a possible suicide mission.

"Lord Bion, what do we do with the runt? He will get in the way or worse. He could be a spy for them. He was told to tell us a sob story to get close to us and Viviana. She will scoop him up like a lost little pup," Anthony voiced his concern as they watched the men leave.

"You have valid points and that is why I will ask Euclid to take him under his wing and teach him some basic knowledge, like math and reading. Plus, the men

123

can keep an eye on him while teaching him some combat skills. He just seems to be too rough to be a spy, but we will watch how he behaves with the group and keep him as far from Viviana as possible. I know his family is loyal to the cause, and I feel I need to do what I can for him and all the people who are having problems on my land. I am responsible." Lord Bion sighed and placed his hand on Anthony's shoulder. "If I have made a mistake, I hope you will be able to do what must be done."

"I will, my lord." Anthony bowed and left Lord Bion as he ordered the men to move the caravan down the road.

As they traveled, Viviana wrote more in her journal. The events of the day were swimming in her mind, and she could not sleep until the details were on the pages. She hoped Marius was doing well with the men. He was a good kid and reminded Viviana of the stable boys, Javius and Mort. She always wanted siblings of her own, but since her father never married again, she had to settle for being a big sister to the children around the Manor.

Once they stopped, she was able to stretch her legs and watch Marius run around with the men. He was swift and sure-footed. She saw him climb a tree and grab some fruit from the vines for Adilynn. Coming down, he glided down off the branches to the ground.

"Marius, would you please bring me water and set it next to the fire?" Viviana watched him struggle with a tree stump sized pot of water. She wanted to help him, but knew he had to show he could do such things on his own and show he was useful. He spilled some but was able to get the pot to her and smile.

"Marius, Euclid is waiting for you," Anthony said in a demanding tone and guided the boy away from Viviana. She watched as they walked away. His voice gave away his mistrust of the lad. Viviana understood why, but she knew in her heart that he just needed the right guidance and support to be a fine young man. Hopefully, he would prove himself strong enough to be one of her father's guards in training. They could use all the loyal men they could find. Perhaps the civil war was years away, but only if Dragoonus did not cross the line with Calestius and drive up the prices of goods in the land. If anything happened to push the people, the war would not only be civil, but it would also stretch to all the neighboring nations.

"You're going to burn the stew, Vi." Adilynn moved the pot from the fire. The flavorful food made everyone eager to sit and eat.

"Enjoy the meal," she said and smiled at the hungry men. She took her food in her tabergo. Viviana was not feeling like being around the crowd. She was lost in thought when Marius found her.

"Please accept this, Lady Bion." He handed her a piece of parchment with 'Thank You' written crudely on it.

"What is this for, lad?"

"You saved me. Euclid said I have a good brain and I can study with him at his house. I will be able to read and write like the masters. My biggest dream has come true. I am forever your servant." He bowed deeply.

"You are not my servant. I did what I would have done for anyone. You deserve education as much as any young mind does. The only thing I want is for you to become an outstanding scholar and teacher. If you do this, your debt to me will be repaid," she said and put her hand under his chin. She raised him from his bow and smiled. His entire face lit up like the sun.

"You have saved me, and I will do the same for you if you ever need it of me." He blushed and ran. She sighed and walked. His sincerity was almost too much for her to bear. She knew he might become troublesome if any other attacks happen. She did not want him getting hurt.

"What did the pup give you?" Anthony's voice said from behind her.

"Just a thank you note, if you must know," she snipped at him. She hated him spying on her.

"I wasn't spying on you, silly girl. I was told to keep an eye on the boy. He is now my charge as well. Between you two, I have no time to do anything else. I don't know if I have enough energy for this," Anthony said, grinning.

"Well, I will make it easier on you tonight. I will be in my tabergo. You can go watch the 'pup' as you like to call him," she said flatly.

"I am sorry, Vi. Aren't we supposed to be able to tease each other?" he asked with a hurt tone. She realized he was trying to make up for before.

"I'm the one who should be sorry. I was curt with you, and that is not fair. You are right about Marius and me. We are a bit of a handful, aren't we?" She smiled and his face lit up, which is when she noticed he was holding something behind his back.

"What, pray tell, are you hiding?" She tried to move behind him to see what he had, but Anthony was quicker than her. She chased him a bit around the tabergo until she was out of breath.

"Done already?" he said quite out of breath too and sat on the tree stump by the fire.

"Yes, you are better at the running game than I, cousin," she said, and he made a sour face at her. "What is that for?"

126

"Nothing, I just wish you would use my name more. I like to hear it from you," Anthony said quietly, so only she could hear him. She blushed deeply, and it made him grin from ear to ear. He then handed her some wildflowers that smelled like the ones in her garden.

"These are beautiful. I should put them in water," she said as she turned away from him. The butterflies flew circles in her stomach with him just standing there. *Is he REALLY doing this to me? I can't have him be so sweet. He is killing me.*

"What is wrong?" His voice snapped her out of her own thoughts.

"Nothing. I need to put these in water." She walked to her tabergo and then turned back to him. "Thank you," she said and touched his hand. He tried to put his other hand on hers, but she moved it and walked away. She kept herself in check until she shut her door and then she flung herself on the bed. The sobbing didn't stop until she was snoring. Sleep was the only escape from her situation with her cousin and her life.

Chapter 16

"Anthony, it's time to get going again. Where is Vi?" Adilynn interrupted her brother's thoughts.

"In her tabergo," he said and dumped the rest of the contents of his bowl.

"No, she isn't," she sounded worried.

"Damn it. I watched her go in and lock the door behind her. I can't protect her if she won't let me!" He growled, which made Adilynn cringe. They quietly searched around the camp but saw no sign of her. They found Remus and had him help them.

"She is safe, but she is very emotional and that makes her dangerous to be around at the moment. I promised her I would keep people away from her until it was time to leave."

"Well, Lord Bion called for us to travel again. He was determined to get her to Euclid's earlier, so she had more time to rest before going to Calestius.

"Then I will go get her. I think she has settled down by now."

"Hopefully," Adilynn said quietly.

"What do you mean, hopefully?" Anthony sounded confused.

"I know how hurtful she can be in one of her bad moods." She showed him her arms above her elbows. She had physical scars from her throwing things and being burned by her hands. "It happened after her mother passed away. I had never seen such pain and agony in one person. When she exploded, I was just too close to her, and this happened."

"I never knew about this. What else are you hiding about Viviana from me?" he asked as he looked at her arms.

"We weren't hiding anything from you. This mood only comes when she becomes emotionally stressed and she does not have a way to vent. Most of the time, she is in control of herself and there is nothing to worry about. However, with her increasing power and the journey, she doesn't have the chance to calm herself. You should leave her be for now. I don't think you want another handprint, or worse this time." Adilynn saw Viviana walking to her tabergo, without looking at anyone. Her eyes were glazed over as if in a trance. Anthony took a step towards her, but his sister stopped him. "Leave her be, brother."

For the next two days, Viviana kept to herself. She was having a terrible time controlling her emotions. She longed for her home, her bed, and her old life, but knew her feelings were more than homesickness. Nothing seemed to brighten her day or make her smile.

Her feelings were becoming darker with each hour. The whole caravan made her mad without speaking a word to her. She wanted to hurt someone or something, and that scared her. She hadn't had such dark thoughts since the attack over a year ago. Viviana knew the journey was taking a toll on part of her body and mind, but nothing could stop her from reaching Calestius, including herself.

"Viviana," Lord Bion called for his daughter.

"Yes, father." She opened her door to him. Her entire demeanor put her father in a distressed state, and it scared him to see her so unbalanced. He asked her to join him at the edge of the woodlands on the side of the road. As they stood there, she could feel the calming aura that emanated from the forest.

"Remus found a slow-moving river with a pool for you deep inside these woods. He will take you there for a few hours. We are on Euclid's land and by midday we will be at the Manor. You can then use all the time you need to balance yourself wholly for the next part of the journey. I knew this might happen with the pressure and hardship of such a travel, but I am glad you will have time before your adventure to Calestius," he said. Viviana knew he was right and once again he knew how to take care of her. She felt depressed, but Remus's voice snapped her out of her thoughts.

"Come with me, little one." He scooped her up in his arms and they left Lord Bion standing there alone. She needed to have a calm heart, and the river would be the best place for her right now.

"Where's Vi and Remus, Uncle?" Anthony sounded worried.

"She needs time to compose herself before meeting with a new group of people. Her nerves are frayed from the journey. She could explode and use her unstable

130

emotions to cause unimaginable destruction. I saw it after her mother died and the attack last year." Lord Bion turned to Anthony. "Please leave her alone with Remus. He is like an uncle to her and knows how to calm her. He also heals quicker than normal people. If he gets hurt, he will be fine. Understand?"

Anthony growled and nodded. He understood, but hated not being by her side protecting her. After leaving Lord Bion, he went to scout the road ahead. He tried to keep his mind away from Viviana, but he couldn't help his thoughts from wandering to his feelings for her. No matter how much he saw of her powers, he still wanted to know more about her. He could see all the sweet and beautiful things about her that made her wonderful. Everyone had their dark side, and he was no exception.

He still could feel the blood on his hands from the men who had stormed the castle. They were farmers and merchants in need of help from their monarch, who would not grant them council. All they wanted was food and help with the crops. They decided to break in and get whatever they could, but only received the steel blades of the king's knights. He could still hear the screams of the men. One grabbed Anthony, trying to stop him from killing another man, but both were slain. They were unarmed and never had a chance against the practiced killers. Anthony still woke with night terrors from that day. He sighed and stared off into the woods, where he noticed movement.

He stopped his horse and saw a shadowy figure the size of a large animal. *Viviana!* His instinct to protect her made him jump off his horse and run towards the sound of flowing water. His heart pounded and legs ached, but he didn't stop until he saw a small pool of water where Remus stood. Anthony felt stupid. Remus was the most likely suspect for the shadow he saw, but at least he could see that Viviana was safe. He wanted to hide, but knew Remus could sense his presence. He slowly approached the pool and saw her. She was entering the water in a beautiful golden dress. Remus stopped Anthony from going any closer to the water. She seemed in some sort of trance. He motioned for Anthony to just watch and observe her.

He was stunned by the pink glow of her beautiful skin. Her eyes burned as if to reflect a fire that could take her over at any moment. She looked at the pool and slowly immersed her entire self under the water. It bubbled and then boil. After a minute, it stopped. Anthony wanted to jump in because he thought she was drowning. Remus put his hand, shoulder and a finger to his lips.

Once the water was completely still, Viviana slowly rose from the pool and looked like herself again. Her eyes were calm sapphires. Her skin was a sun-kissed honey color. Her wet clothes and hair were clinging to her curvy body. Anthony couldn't keep his jaw from dropping. She looked at Remus and then Anthony. She wanted to feel embarrassed, but the look on his face made her almost giggle. Knowing her state of dress caught him by surprise, she felt better than calm at that moment. She was at peace with herself and now could safely continue the journey.

"What was that?" Anthony asked as he placed a robe around her arms. She smiled and shrugged.

"I used the most complicated calming technique I know to wash away my anger, frustration and anxiety so they would stop controlling me."

"So, without that...?" he asked with concern in his voice.

"I would have either set the forest on fire or killed someone... maybe even the whole traveling party. The feelings hit with such force that I needed to do something to release and cleanse my body and mind. I'm hoping at the Shrine they will have something more powerful since this time I boiled the water."

"That's not normal?" Anthony and Remus said at the same time.

"Nope, and it was harder to get the feelings released. I fear what might happen if I can't control this power." She looked at the men as her legs shook. Anthony grabbed her arm to steady her, but she was too weak to stand. He wanted to scoop her up, but Remus moved quicker and bent down.

"Here," Remus said and hoisted her up onto his back. She held onto his shoulders as he carried her back to the camp, sobbing silently all the way to the camp.

When they returned to the rest of the group, they all seemed ready to leave. Lord Bion quickly and quietly guided Viviana to her tabergo and gave her a crushing bear hug.

"I am going to miss you, daughter." The sadness in his voice made Viviana's eyes swell with more tears than before. They would be parting soon. She hugged him back with all her strength and gave him a big smile. He left so she could sleep while they finished their journey to Euclid's mansion.

"Time to head out," Lord Bion shouted, and started the caravan traveling again. In just a few hours, they would be safe, and all could clean the dust from their bodies and lay their heads on soft beds. Everyone was looking forward to a home cooked meal and clean sheets.

Chapter 17

As the day moved towards night, the horses pulled the caravan faster and faster toward the mansion in the distance. The vast house made of gray and white stone stood ready for guests. The windows were open to let the last breezes of summer in, and the smell of baking bread filled the air around the courtyard. The caravan arrived just before sunset and Euclid's parents greeted the guests at the door.

"Please let the stable boys take the horses and everyone come inside. We have a feast ready for you all. If you wish to wash before dinner, please follow the maids to the second floor. There is enough warm water for all." His face lit up at the sight of his son and daughter-in-law. He then saw Lord Bion. "Ah, Lord Bion, my friend. I am so glad to see you are in good health. I hope the trip was uneventful?"

"Oh, it was quite eventful, but everyone is alive and safe at the moment. I fear though the queen knows Viviana is still alive, and she will not stop her attacks.

The last one had thieves, bandits, and poor farmers as the attackers."

"That is quite a low blow to use such tactics. Did they get to Viviana?"

"No, but they used a boy from a farming family I know well as their scout and guide. Since I know his family, I granted him the chance to prove himself as a student to Euclid and a servant to this house. He wants to help his family and work off his debt to me."

"Ah, so he just needed money for his family?"

"Yes," Lord Bion looked around him as he spoke.

"Well, this is Euclid's house and if he wants to help this boy, he will. I am just happy that no one was hurt or killed during this event. I am hoping things will stay quiet here while all the company rests weary bones."

"I hope so, too. My bones are reminding me just how old I am and how this world will soon be in the hands of our young ones. They will be our leaders, our brave fighters, and thinkers. It is a heavy weight we must place on them. I hope they will handle such pressure when their destiny comes to light." Lord Bion let out a deep sigh and let his friend lead the way to the banquet hall while the rest of the travelers went to wash up and rest before the party started.

Viviana only cleaned herself up a bit and went to her room. She had bathed in the river and still felt refreshed. However, her wardrobe was not. Her cousin had many fine dresses from her wedding, and she hoped Adilynn would let her wear one for the dinner feast.

When she reached Adilynn, she heard her talking to Anthony in a concerned voice. It was difficult to make out what exactly they , but both seemed flustered and mad at each other. She didn't want to interrupt, but she wanted to change, so she knocked loudly to let them know she was there.

"Vi, how are you doing? Did you need something?" Adilynn sounded upbeat, but she still looked shaky. Anthony bowed and left the room without a word to Viviana. It seemed as if there was something weighing heavy on his shoulders, and it made her nervous about the rest of the journey.

"Well, first you can tell me what that was all about, and I need a proper dress for tonight. I have nothing to wear." Viviana tried to sound nonchalant.

"Oh, you know how crazy paranoid Anthony gets about parties since your last one. He is very much against you going downstairs tonight and wants to keep you in your room until tomorrow. I told him that only family and very close friends would be here tonight. This town is quite smaller than uncle's and we are very well protected by many of Euclid's old buddies from school. As for the dress, I have several I want to give you since it will be many months before I can wear them again." Adilynn smiled as she saw the look on Viviana's face.

"I'm going to have a new cousin?" she squealed.

"Well, we are hoping." She held her stomach. "I realized a few days into the journey that I have not had my monthly cycle and that is a likely sign. Plus, I want you to be known as our baby's aunt. You are the closest person I have to a sister, and no one will spoil this child more than you!" She hugged Viviana and started to cry.

"I promise I will be back to give this child all the toys and sweets I can. You just have to take care of yourself and this house. I am so excited for you," she said through her own tears. She hated she had to leave Adilynn in such a state, but she will have her mother-in-law and even her own mother in a few months. She will miss being able to

136

see her grow and change into a beautiful mother. The emotions made them a little late for dinner, but no one except Lord Bion and Euclid seem to notice.

"How are you two doing?" Euclid asked, but did not need words to figure out what had kept the ladies. He smiled and took his blushing wife in his arms. "We should make the announcement before Viviana says anything," he said loud enough for her to hear him. She stuck her tongue out at him and went to her seat.

"Actually, I want to wait until we are sure. Once I know, we will make the announcement. Vi, you and Anthony are the only ones who know anything."

"Your secret is safe with me." She hugged her cousin and walked down with them to dinner.

The feast started with a flavorful tray of cheeses and fruit from all over the continent. Some of them Viviana never tasted before, but she was feeling adventurous and tried them all. Only one fruit was too potent for her taste buds and made her spit it out in a napkin. She felt a little embarrassed about acting like such a child, but it made her feel better when her father did the same thing. He smiled at her and they both knew what each other had done without words. These were the many reasons why she would miss his company terribly. She looked to Adilynn and Euclid and saw the love between them. Her mood was cheerful with a dash of sadness. She took a breath and pushed away every feeling but excitement. Viviana was determined to enjoy her last few days of being with her family.

"This is how you need to celebrate everything in life. Dancing, wonderful food, and amazing family!" Viviana said into Adilynn's ear.

"This is what we will do for you when you come home! We will make the hall of our home and your home ring for weeks when you return. I love you, sis. You take care of my brother. I know there are feelings between you two… I can see it when you are around each other," Adilynn said and noted that Viviana blushed a deep rose color. She had no idea that Adilynn had noticed anything, since she was always with Euclid. "Please, both of you come home soon. I need you and him, and so does the possible new addition to the family."

"And so does my father," Viviana said remembering the sobering fact that she would leave him soon.

"May I cut in?" Cornelius appeared from nowhere.

"It's fine," Viviana said and hugged her cousin sweetly, like she was a frail porcelain doll. Adilynn hugged her back with such force it almost took her breath away and then went back to her husband.

"Shall we?" He offered her his hand, which she took, and they started dancing.

"So, I see you are enjoying yourself and no one has tried to kill us yet. I am impressed so far."

"I feel safe here. No reports of intruders as of late. It will be between here and the border. We will have to stay alert for attacks."

"Ah," he leaned in closer to her and whispered, "You are so sweet and naïve. You need to have more skepticism for your safety. My despicable mother is quite predictable, and she will send more men out for you and me. She can use me as a catalyst for war if they find me dead with the revolutionaries or use me as a puppet on the throne. Neither I really care for. You, I can see as a superb weapon or a prominent leader. Either way, you are vital to her plans, and she is ruthless. Mother will get what she wants. Why do you think my father's first wife died?" He grinned in such a way that it stunned Viviana for a moment. She saw Anthony and met his green-as-summer-grass eyes. He seemed tipsy from the mead, but also frustrated to see her in the arms of his arch nemesis. Moving quickly through the crowd, he stopped and stood in front of the couple.

"May I cut in?" he asked in a polite but slightly angry tone.

"Of course," Cornelius bowed out and left the two to dance.

"So how are you enjoying the party and the news of a possible new addition to the family?" she asked quietly. Viviana tried to make him smile, but it did not work. It seemed to make his mood worse.

"I am happy, but it kills me to know we have to leave them… to leave Adilynn when she is in such a state. I can't protect her from what is coming with…"

"With the war? Father said that unless the queen declares war on Calestius, the revolt will stay quiet until I get back. Father believes that with my power and leadership abilities, I will be the key to taking down the king… or I guess I should say the queen. We will be back in time for the precious bundle of joy to get to know us and we will make this land safe for him or her." She knew it sounded too sweet and idealistic, but these were her wishes. He pulled her closer to him and embraced her with such sweetness and tenderness that she felt she would melt in his arms.

"Please be careful of what Cornelius tells you though. He is here for one reason, to save his own skin," he said, and she pulled away from him.

"I know you feel concerned for me, but he is as well. He said his mother would not stop until she had both of us in her possession. I believe he is right. Hopefully, we are safe here, but I will heed his warning. I hope you will do the same." She bowed, and he left her standing on the dance floor.

As she watched Anthony walk away from the hall, she felt a twinge of guilt for upsetting him. She knew the history between the two men and understood him wanting to protect her from the prince. However, she also felt he might be jealous of her talking to another man as well. She shook her head and went to find her father.

Her search came to a halt when a dashing young man found her. He resembled the boy they picked up in the woods. She smiled at him as he handed her a beautiful, thornless red rose and bowed gracefully.

"It would be a great honor to have this dance with you, Lady Viviana." His eloquent proposal took her by surprise.

"It would be my honor to dance with such a handsome young gentleman like yourself, Sir Marius." She gave him a deep curtsy. He blushed and quickly took her hand. They proceeded to the dance floor and joined in a jovial and quite spirited spin around the floor. The entire hall was losing energy as the dance ended.

"I believe I should say goodnight, sir. I am quite exhausted from dancing and feasting." She didn't want to hurt his feelings since he looked like he wanted another dance, but she was about to pass out from the extremely long day.

"I agree. I am quite tired, too. I think Master Euclid and Lady Adilynn have retired for the night. Would you allow me to walk you to your room?" He was such a quick study and learned in a short time how to be a very well-spoken and charming young man.

"Well, since my guard is missing, I will take you up on your offer." Viviana hooked her arm around his elbow, and he guided her to say goodnight to her father. Then they went up the stairs to the second floor to her guest room. She wished she were several years younger because Marius would be a wonderful suitor. He reminded her of when Gavius tried to woo her. He was just as charming and handsome. A little wave of homesickness washed over her, but it passed as they continued down the hallway.

She listened to Marius tell her about his lessons when they heard shouting. Anthony's voice hit her ears, and she turned to see a man dressed in black garb coming at them. His face was covered with a black sash, and he held a thin, long blade made to pierce the heart. Viviana moved to guard Marius, but he pushed her out of the way as the man thrust the blade into the boy's heart. The weapon went straight through him, and Viviana let out a blood-curdling scream.

Pulling the knife out of Marius' body, the butcher turned to attack her next. He stabbed at her, but the blade landed on the palm of her hand. The man tried to push through her flesh, but the metal melted to the hilt in front of the attacker's eyes. He took one look into her eyes and froze. Flames of red, orange, and blue danced in her once sapphire eyes. She reached out to him and touched his chest. The scream from his lips pierced the night. As he crumbled to the ground, his eyes, nose, and mouth leaked blood and steam rose from his limp and charred body.

She then turned to see another man dressed the same with a bigger sword coming towards her. A sinister smile crossed her lips as the man ran at her. This time, she used the fire in the torches on the wall to deliver his fate. Pointing to the walls, she beckoned the flame to do her bidding. They leapt from the torches and swirled above the man's head. In a swift motion, she brought her hands together and then down towards the ground. The flames obeyed her and engulfed the man. His screams of pain rang through the hallways as he ran past Viviana.

She felt unhinged. Her eyes found Marius' body and her heart broke again. Letting out an animalistic howl, she dropped to the floor. Anthony followed the sound and found her with the bodies in the hallway.

"Oh, god," he said as he choked. Viviana saw him hold his breath and stomach for a moment as to center himself. She heard him shout her name, but she could not hold on any longer and the hall went dark.

Chapter 18

"What's going on?" Viviana woke up feeling the warmth of someone's breath on her head and her body being jostled about. The smell of smoke lingered on her clothes, and she panicked.

"It's going to be alright, Vi. You're safe with me." Anthony's voice made her grab his hands and grip them. She felt a belt around her waist and realized that he had put it around them to keep her from falling while they rode away from Euclid's Manor.

"How many were there?" she asked, trying to hold back the tears welling up in her eyes.

"I am not sure, but I took out one, and you took down two. I found a camp in the woods that had only one there. Their garb and weapons belong to a small country north of Dragoonus known for their trained assassins." He slowed down the horse and looked back to where they came to listen for any movement.

"Where is the camp?" She tried not to get angry.

"It's destroyed. I made sure of it, after I…"

"After what?"

"There is a spot just over there that we can sit and rest for now. Remus will come get us soon." He guided the horse over to a small clearing where a fire once burned. Viviana shivered as she waited for Anthony to dismount. He went to give her a hand, but she swung her leg over and landed swiftly on her feet. She could see his smile in the moonlight, but then she noticed his leg and his arms covered in blood.

"My word, what happened?" she said as he leaned against a tree. Viviana saw the smile vanish. The pain and anger on his face made her worried.

"When I found the camp, the assassin caught me off guard and got me in the leg with his dagger." He stiffened as she placed her hand on his leg. Viviana worked her hand gently on the wound and breathed.

"Tell me more," she said as she looked at the rest of his leg.

"We fought, and I killed him. More blood is on my hands now."

"More?" Her eyes met his, and he cringed.

"There is so much you do not know about me... I wish I could erase it all."

"We both have blood on our hands, Anthony. Darkness has touched both of us, but do we let it rule us? Have we let it burn itself in our hearts?" she asked, with tears running down her face.

"You are sweeter and kinder than anyone I have ever met, Vi. Even with the power you wield, you only want to protect those you love. Even when the darkness calls to you, you fight it." He smiled. "Besides, I would not be alive without you."

"But Marius would be alive if not for me," she sobbed as Anthony held her.

"We make a fine pair, don't we?" The way he said that last line made her blush. She pushed herself away from him and straightened up, wiping the tears away.

"What about the others?" She didn't want to think about them being alone in the woods.

"I warned them before I found you. They should have everything under control now." He stood and helped Viviana up.

"Thanks for the leg." He touched her cheek and just like that, his eyes closed, and he went down to his knees. Viviana kept him from hitting his head as he convulsed and foamed at the mouth.

"Poison. Oh, no. I don't know what to do," she said as she held his head in her lap. "Think, Vi! What do you have?" Then it hit her. "Blood," she said out loud, but she didn't know if it would work on poison. "Only one way to know." She pricked her finger and held Anthony's mouth open just enough to get a few drops in. He breathed heavier, and his eyes twitched. Her heart ached to see him in pain, but there was nothing she could do.

"Viviana, there you are. What in the world…"

"He was poisoned. I've tried everything I can. What can we do, Remus?" she cried out as she watched Anthony struggle to breathe. Viviana placed her hands on him and let out a terrifying scream as her hands glowed with a purple hue. She could feel the poison in her fingers as they tingled with pain. Pushing herself, Viviana continued to keep her hands on him. The tingling in her hands moved up her arms and to her chest. Breathing became difficult, and she feared passing out.

"Vi, don't!" Remus' voice seemed distant and fuzzy. She felt his hands on her shoulders, but she couldn't let go until Anthony was saved. His life was in her hands again.

"Let go!" another familiar voice said.

"Father," she cried out as she took her hands off of Anthony. Lord Bion ran to her side and held her in his arms as she convulsed in pain. Her eyes flowed with tears as she looked at Anthony.

"He is breathing, Vi. You must concentrate on you." Remus watched as she closed her eyes.

"Here, let me help." Cornelius' voice made her open her eyes. He placed his hands on hers and focused on her. The pain subsided from her hands, and she could breathe easier.

"That's all I can do," he said as he shook his hands. "They are tingling. The poison..." was the last thing Viviana heard before she passed out.

Chapter 19

Viviana awoke with a start as she looked around and saw she was in bed. The warmth of the sun filtered through the window, and she felt well rested. She took a deep breath and smiled. Her lungs were healed. Stretching out her hands and arms, the tingling sensation was gone.

"I see you are awake, lazybones." Adilynn's chipper voice was a stark contrast to her disheveled look. Her eyes were puffy and red from crying, it seemed.

"You poor thing. You should rest," Viviana said as she rose from the bed, steadying herself. Her legs were still a little weak from the poisoning.

"Don't get up. There is no need for you to move until you are completely healed." She tried to force Viviana to lie back down, but she would do no such thing.

"Adri, I'm fine. The only thing I need is a bath and fresh clothes. How is Anthony doing?"

"You can ask him yourself," Adilynn said as her brother walked in. Viviana blushed as he bowed to her.

"Once again, you have saved my life, Viviana. I can never repay you for this," he said as his voice crackled. "However, I believe that you will be happ…"

"Marius!" Viviana cried as the young man poked his head from behind Anthony. He ran to her, but stopped and dropped to his knees.

"I am so glad to see you are well, Lady Viviana." He looked up at her with a smile. He did not have a chance to move as Viviana wrapped her arms around him and cried on his shoulder.

"Ah, one big happy family reunion," Cornelius said as he walked into the room. "Looks like you didn't get everyone killed after all."

"Shut up, you vile cretin!" Anthony grabbed Cornelius' collar.

"Please don't." Viviana's voice made Anthony let go and back away.

"You should have more control over your mongrel." Cornelius straightened his shirt.

"She could say the same thing about mine," Aurora said as she entered the room. Her voice had lost its sweetness and made Cornelius move towards the window.

"My love, you are so cruel to me." He, but she continued to give him a deadly look.

"I am happy to see you are awake and well. Marius, you, and the men go downstairs. Let Lord Bion and Lord Euclid know Lady Viviana is up. We will see to getting her ready for the day. Thank you." Her voice was firm but kind towards the young man. He gave her a quick bow and moved to the door. Anthony and Cornelius followed without a word.

"Thank you. The room was getting a little crowded." Viviana smiled, even with tears still in her eyes.

"How is your body doing?" Aurora asked.

"My legs are a bit weak, but other than that, I seem to be back to normal. Thank heavens Anthony and Marius are alive." She sat on the bed and dried her eyes.

"We were lucky that the house did not catch on fire any more than it did. I know you are beating yourself up, Vi, but you saved many people the other night," said Adilynn as she sat by her.

"Other night? How long was I out?"

"Almost three days. You had us worried. Even with Cornelius lending a hand, it still took a toll on you." Aurora sat in a chair by the window.

"That's right. He helped heal me." Viviana smiled when she remembered him being chivalrous.

"Not precisely. He just used his very limited ability to take some of the poison from your body. Cornelius had no one to help him sharpen the gifts he has, so they are nothing compared to yours. He feels a little lost right now. I think that's why he wanted to do something for you. He is convinced that you are related somehow." Aurora looked at Viviana. Viviana didn't know what to say to that and just shrugged.

"Well, I still need to thank him for his help. It might have taken me longer to heal without him. Now, how in the world is Marius still alive? I watched the sword go through his heart!" She looked at Adilynn and then at Aurora.

"The funny thing is that the blade did not strike his heart. It went just above it and to the side. He was bleeding terribly, but Cornelius found him and took him to the healing house. We have quite a few talented healers here." Adilynn smiled as she went to find Viviana something to wear from the trunk in the room.

"We should hurry downstairs. The tabergos are ready if Viviana can travel. I hate to rush, but time is not on our side." Aurora moved towards the door. "If you two can manage without me, I want to finish tying up some loose ends."

"Of course, Aurora. We will be down as soon as I have washed up and changed. Thank you for everything."

"It is nothing, your ladyship. If you will excuse me." Aurora curtsied and left the room.

"What was that about?" Viviana asked Adilynn as she moved to the warm water sitting in the basin. She washed up as she waited for an answer.

"We have titles, Vi. I know it's hard for you to remember, but you *are* a lord's daughter, and I am a lord's wife. Aurora comes from the palace, and I think it's a sign of respect."

"I don't know. It seems so forced. She was calling us by our names when we were not here."

"Just let it go, Vi."

"What happened, Adri?"

"Just...."

"What?"

"Your father reminded Cornelius and Aurora yesterday of their place in this group. Cornelius was being pompous, and Lord Bion couldn't take it anymore. He said some things that might be considered threats," Adilynn said sheepishly.

"That man! I swear. If it is not one thing, it's another. He's as bad as Anthony." Viviana stopped talking.

"Vi, you need to be careful around them. I am still not comfortable with their company and would hate to see you get hurt more than you already have." She handed her a towel and helped her dress.

"I will," she put on her shoes and grabbed Adilynn's arm. They walked down to the hall where everyone had gathered. The smell of lemon water and roses greeted Viviana's nose as she noticed the missing tapestry.

"Ah, I see you can walk again. Now maybe we can get started. I'm not really keen on being stuck with this group any longer than we need to." Cornelius snagged an apple from the table and stood there, waiting for a response.

"And here I was going to thank you for helping me. But instead," she threw him a deadly look, "the feelings are mutual, you royal pain in the ass!" Viviana said, and everyone just stared at her. "I, personally, have been through hell the past day or so and would like to be free of anyone that might bring any more problems, prince!" She stormed out. Of course, she insulted Cornelius enough that he became furious.

"No one talks to me like that! You are not the only person who has suffered, you brat. My Aurora and I barely made it out of the mansion before the fire..." He stopped.

"What?" she roared.

"Well, one assassin ran through the hall on fire and caught some drapes on fire. I'm surprised the Manor is still standing. No thanks to you, you menace."

"Cornelius, would you just shut up!" Aurora punched his bicep as hard as she could, and he flinched. He made a pained expression at her and she rolled her eyes. Everyone looked at them until Viviana started laughing.

"I'm sorry, but I just couldn't help it. I'm sorry Cornelius. You are right. I am still not under control and could cause more damage than what I already have to your new home." She gave everyone a sad smile and tried not to cry again. Tears were useless.

"Vi, stop beating yourself up over it. Those men could have killed everyone here. The fire damage is minimal, and everyone is safe." Euclid hugged her. His warmth made her feel better.

"I hate to say it, but we should get on the road." Anthony stood close to the doorway. Viviana could sense he was anxious to get moving again.

"You are right, Anthony. Let's move out to the stables." Lord Bion motioned for Viviana to take his arm. She did and allowed him to guide her outside. Remus was sitting by in the shade of a tall oak tree. Viviana waved to him, but he seemed to be deep in thought. It was not until she saw ruffling feathers she knew he was listening to Master Oryn talk. She could just make out the owl looking bird perched on a branch close to Remus' head.

"I am sorry to say this, but it still does not look safe from attacks, and I fear it may happen again soon. We will create a diversion by taking a tabergo with the prince and Aurora on the main road. You, Anthony, and Remus will travel to the border through the forest. During the night we will find each other and rest together," Master Oryn pointed to the woods.

"Wouldn't it be safer to stay on the main road? Bandits and thieves roam the woods. Besides, I feel like a coward hiding. They will find me either way. At least we can all have our guard up and fight for each other. I don't want anyone being my decoy," she said vehemently.

"Well, I guess the lady has made a valid point. I hope you are ready for what might happen. Not only are there assassins but also all the kingdom's guards are looking for you," Master Oryn said and jumped on a horse.

"They are looking for Viviana, daughter of Lord Bion. I am now Cleo of Crestine, who is a teacher traveling to Calestius for work. My paperwork is all in order and so is Anthony's. You are Gavius."

"Wait, a minute! I am who?" He was furious.

"I had to think of something that would allow us to keep our cover of traveling through father's land. If we say anything about that area, then it will be because you are from there. You are Gavius, a hired bodyguard, to escort me through Dragoonus and Calestius."

"We only use these names then?" he grumbled as they readied for travel.

"So, I guess I will stick to the forest. I don't think you can explain me," Remus chuckled. Viviana smiled, but did not like the idea of him being alone out there.

"I see by that look you dislike this arrangement. I shall go with him and keep him company. I don't think it would be easy to explain my place in this group. We will find you at nightfall to help with protecting our precious cargo." Master Oryn winked at Viviana, and she smiled.

The feeling of dread left as they moved. She was ready to face her future, no matter what it held. Her father was safe and would be back home by the time they reached Calestius. This made her journey more bearable. Being with Anthony and the others also helped her relax about the uncertainty she felt about all the dangers that awaited them.

Chapter 20

The day was still warm as Viviana sat by Anthony's side, since he was her 'guard,' enjoying the breeze as they traveled along the road. The story made sense if the knights didn't think too hard about it. His anger about his character was making her a little sad, though. She wanted to talk to him and have him make her laugh like he did before. No matter how hard she tried, he still was grumpy about the name she picked.

"Gavius?" Viviana tried to make it sound casual.

"What?" he growled.

"Would you like a drink of water?" She tried to be as nice as possible. She knew how he felt, but he had to deal with it for the next few days.

"No thanks, Vi… Cleo," he said with a stutter. He seemed to not like that name but wouldn't tell Viviana why. It made her a little upset, because she had always liked that name and used it frequently to name her cats.

"Adonius, how are you and Aliana doing?" she called back to the couple.

"We are fine; just try not to jostle us so much." As usual, the prince was being his charming self. Viviana rolled her eyes and swore to herself that she would teach the prince a lesson if he kept being rude to them. She wished they could move faster, but the horses would tire out too easily if they quickened the pace. Even if they could get to the border in less time, they still were stuck with the royal brat and Aurora. At their current rate, they would reach the border in two days and then it would be two more to the Sun Shrine. She would hopefully celebrate her twenty-first birthday in Calestius with no more incidents.

As she pondered her future at the Shrine, she noticed Anthony looked quite tense. She saw the muscles in his jaw and cheeks tighten and relax as his eyes darted side to side. His level of alertness made her quite nervous, which made her question what was out there that he wasn't telling her about.

"Would you relax a little? You are making me nervous," she said, trying to snap him out of it.

"Someone is following us. I can feel it. I don't know why, but someone's out there." Anthony shook his shoulders, trying to loosen his muscles.

"Well, Remus and Master Oryn are out there," she said.

"Thank you for stating the obvious. I know that, but I feel like I am being stalked like prey. It's not them."

"So, we will tell them about your feeling and see what they think. Remus would warn us if someone was out there, or he would take care of it. Either way, all assassins are dead or too scared to come after us. Remember? I set one on fire and boiled one from the inside out. I would think it would make anyone think twice about coming after me," she said with a smile on her face, but seriousness in her voice. It scared her knowing what she could do, and it made Anthony uncomfortable when she mentioned it. He shifted the reins and moved a little farther away from her. She knew he didn't do it purposely, but the actions hurt her.

She tried not to show it, but her whole mood changed. She watched the trees and said nothing for several hours as they made their way to the border. He yawned a little, and she shivered. He moved closer to her, without looking at her. She pulled her blanket up to her arms and put her head on his shoulder. They were both exhausted from the ride and needed sleep.

"We should make the others give up the tabergo so we can get some rest," he said and then blushed. He mumbled something under his breath.

"It would be fine with me, but it might look improper."

"I know. I'm a moron. I shouldn't have…"

"It's fine. I know what you meant and quite honestly, there is enough room for two separate cots." Viviana just wanted a way to lie down without stopping.

"That's true. Then we could keep going into the night. I want off the road as soon as possible." He was reading her mind,, and she smiled.

"Remus," she called out, and the bear-like creature appeared from nowhere and spooked the horses.

"Hey!" A shout made the three cringe. None of them wanted to hear any whining from the prince.

"He will regret any snide comment he makes," Anthony said loud enough for Cornelius to hear.

"Excuse you! I just wanted to know why we stopped." He sounded concerned and annoyed by Anthony's remark.

156

"I am tired and so is my guard. I think switching would allow us to continue into the night and let us get some sleep."

"Not a good idea." Remus said, trying not to give away his feelings on that idea.

"We need to set up camp every night, so we are not attacked on the road. I can't protect you out there." Remus looked at Viviana.

"You are right, but I want the tabergo for us tonight. We both need sleep." Viviana could hear the intake of air from everyone.

"It's not proper." Anthony made the statement that everyone wanted to say.

"I don't care. I am feeling the same way about being stalked and I need you to be close." Viviana shivered.

"What is that about?" Remus looked at Anthony.

"There are eyes, well-trained eyes, on us. I have felt them since we got on the road."

"Well, I have sensed nothing, but it doesn't mean the threat is not there," Master Oryn said, and Remus nodded. "Anthony was a high-ranking knight and a well-trained tracker. We will keep an extra set of eyes out tonight. Cornelius and Aurora can take the first watch. We will stay close but hidden in the woods." Remus started helping set up camp.

Before everyone settled down for the evening, Viviana made dinner. As the group ate, they kept their guard up. Anthony still felt the eyes of a stalker on them. He sat right by Viviana like a guard dog. She didn't say it, but it made her happy to have him so close.

"Here." Anthony handed her a piece of bread and their hands touched, which made her pulse race.

"Thank you," she said. Sitting next to him made her nervous and flustered, so she tried to focus on her food.

157

However, her mind wandered to her feelings for him. He was a wonderful man, but she knew what she felt came from his loyalty and protection of her. She just hoped he would lose interest afterward, too. From her experience, unrequited love makes people mean and hurtful.

"Hey, what are you thinking?" His voice made her focus on his handsome face. She blushed and shrugged.

"What?" he asked.

"Just girly thoughts, nothing you would find interesting," she mumbled. "I think it's time for some sleep. Goodnight." She washed out her bowl and disappeared into the comfort and solitude of the tabergo.

"I will be right here if you need me," he said, trying to reassure her.

"Thank you. I will be fine. Please be safe." She closed the door and lit a candle. The bed looked so inviting, but her heart skipped a beat when she thought of sleeping. They were just a day or so away from the border, and a sense of dread was lodged in her mind. She lay down and started counting sheep, only getting to five before she was snoring.

"No!" she yelled as she awoke and looked around. The sun lit the tabergo, and she saw Aurora out cold in the other bed. She mumbled something and started snoring again. Viviana didn't realize how exhausted her body was until she went to bed. Then it hit her: the dread was back. She flung open the door to see the Remus cooking. She sighed and smiled. No one was hurt. The night went smoothly with no attacks. Everyone trusted Anthony, but nothing happened, and she wondered if the group would start doubting him. Maybe he was simply paranoid. Viviana hoped not, but she was also sick and tired of people trying to kill her and wished for a safe trip to the border.

"Vi, how did you sleep?" Remus saw the confused look on her face when she saw the men on the ground.

"How are the boys?" She could see them breathing heavy.

"They stayed up as long as they could, but I assured them no one was out there, and they finally fell asleep. I almost had to knock Anthony out myself, but once their heads hit the pillow, they were sleeping like babes. Master Oryn and I kept watch until now. I think we will rest after you all get going again. I told the young men to keep you ladies hidden. If anyone attacks, you can hide out and surprise the attackers if needed. You two lovely women are just as strong as your traveling companions," Remus smiled.

"You would know, Remus. Just be careful. If someone is following us, they might notice if you two are missing."

"I am hoping for it. I didn't want to worry Anthony and Cornelius. I think Anthony is right. I caught a slight odor in the air, and it didn't seem to fit with everything else around here. If we stay behind, maybe they will show up and we can take care of the danger before they get to you."

"Ah, good plan Remus. Just be careful. If it took this long for you to detect whoever is out there, it might be a trap to get rid of you and Master Oryn. Divide and conquer. It's one of the best battle strategies out there. Father talked about the great battles and how they were won…"

"… and lost," Anthony added.

"Guess you weren't sleeping as solid as you appeared." Master Oryn walked out of the forest with firewood.

159

"I caught what I needed to know. And thank you, Remus. You were right doing that for me. It would have been very difficult to go to sleep knowing that information," he said sheepishly.

"Truth hurts sometimes," Remus said, and patted him on the head.

"Go ahead and wake sleeping beauty and let's get camp packed up. We will follow you back to the road and then find a resting place. A bird will come to you to signal that we are back on your trail," Master Oryn said.

"A bird? What type?" Viviana did not know what kind he could find to send them a message.

"It won't have a message for you, but it will be the message. You will definitely know it is from me." He smiled and all of them looked at him oddly. Viviana had an idea of what he would send, and she said nothing to the others. She smiled, thinking about the possible looks on everyone's face when Master Oryn sent his message. Viviana hoped no one would try to attack him like last time. She stopped smiling when they reached the road. Her fears were surfacing again, even with protecting the tabergo.

"One more day," she said to herself.

"About that… might need one more night so we don't wear out the horses or the boys," Aurora spoke up from her position at the window. "I know this is for our safety, but I hate feeling caged."

"I know the feeling. I have felt that way since I can remember." Viviana looked out her window.

"Please. You know nothing of the solitude of being locked up like an animal," Aurora snapped, and then sighed. "Sorry."

"You were imprisoned?"

"When I first arrived out of Calestius, they said I stole food from a small town, but in truth I turned down the advances of the fruit merchant. I had to escape without being seen or I could not complete my mission." Aurora looked as if she was thinking about those days.

"To spy on the kingdom?"

"And to win the heart of a prince or knight."

"You did both," Vi said and bit her lip. "Sorry, that was mean."

Aurora just smiled. "You are right, though. I caught two, but only one caught mine fully. I didn't even know he was a prince."

"What?"

"In fact, he lied to me when we first met in the marketplace. He's very good with disguises and I thought he was a fabric merchant. We saw each other a few times,, and that's when I broke it off with Anthony. I started falling for a humble, sweet, and kind merchant, which was not a part of my plan. Then I saw the truth when I saw him at the palace on my first day there. He apologized for hours after that, but we had to keep up the other identity, so his mother did not find out about us. I am really sorry about hurting Anthony, but you do not pick who you fall in love with. Just don't tell Anthony about all of it. He has suffered enough by my hand." Viviana could hear the sincerity in her voice and agree to say nothing of the story to him.

"You're right. You cannot choose who you love, but some things just cannot be. I am glad it worked for you." She turned from Aurora and listened to the hooves pound the dirt on the road.

The women sat in silence as the horses continued to the border that was supposed to be neutral territory, but everyone knew no such place existed. Once across, the border patrol wouldn't be able to touch them.

"They still could shoot at us… if they wound us… what if the border patrol is on the Dragoonus' payroll? We won't be safe until we get to the Sun Shrine!" Cornelius' voice was loud and angry.

"We are going to protect you and Viviana. Aurora may be a 'precious flower' to you, but I know what she is capable of, and she can fight men ten times bigger than she is. I've seen it. She told me you have information for Queen Loviana, and Viviana is vital to the revolt as well. Nothing will stop us from our duties to our countries. I made the needed modifications to the tabergo like you said and Master Oryn said the queen's personal guards will get us to the Sun Shrine. I seriously doubt any of the men in Calestius are working for your mother," Anthony said firmly.

"Food," Viviana said, handing them a basket from the front side window close to Anthony. They thanked her and went back to silence.

"By the way, we can hear both of you and if anyone can take care of themselves, I would think it would be me. Last time I checked; I can manipulate fire." She closed the window and left the men speechless.

"Well, you just put them in their place," Aurora said and giggled. Viviana smiled.

"I haven't seen a proper smile on your face before." Viviana took a bite of her apple.

"Smiling isn't something I have much time for unless Cornelius and I are alone. He knows how to make me comfortable enough to smile and laugh."

"Anthony does that sometimes," Viviana said without thinking.

"I know it's a bit taboo, but you two would make a great couple. He smiles a lot around you and he's very protective of you," Aurora said, making Viviana very uncomfortable.

"We only feel for each other because of his charge to protect me. It's sweet and romantic, but it will disappear when he is done with his duty." She stared out the window.

"Ah, so that is how you think Anthony works? He would have broken many hearts if that were how he worked. He has only fallen for two women that I know of and neither of them was weak, frail, or superficial. Anthony only has eyes for a woman who is strong, sweet, and fierce. One who needs a companion in life, not a man to save her all the time. I see how he looks at you..."

"Please stop. He's my cousin and even if only by law, we are not meant to be!" Vi turned away from Aurora.

"By law?" Aurora asked.

"I'm not supposed to talk about it." Viviana bit her lip and said no more. They sat in silence as the tabergo continued down the road.

Chapter 21

Viviana tried to lie down and quiet her mind by listening to the sound of the wheels moving slowly down the dirt road. She meditated, but the sound of the men arguing made her head ache. She opened the small window close to them and growled. Anthony and Cornelius jumped at the sound and turned to see Viviana. They smiled like two boys caught by their mother.

"Aurora is sleeping and I'm meditating. No arguing! No fighting! Do not disturb us with your childish behavior," she said and then shut the window with force. She made her point quite clear.

"I should have known that was coming," Anthony said to himself.

"Well, if you would stop talking about strategies and annoying me to death," Cornelius grumbled.

"Don't say another word to me or mumble to yourself. If we don't talk, then we should be able to stay civil." Anthony kept his eyes on the road.

As the silence grew longer, the men noticed the trees swaying with a warm breeze and they were inching closer to the end of their journey. In the distance, they saw a small town snuggled at the base of a massive wall. The stone structure looked worn and aged by centuries of weather.

"We need to make camp," Anthony said as he slowed down and looked for a place to rest. He stopped in a clearing off from the road and stretched his body. He nudged Cornelius, who grumbled at him.

"I was doing just fine. Why are we stopping?"

"It will be dark soon. I could keep going to town, but the guards are on higher alert at night than during the day." Anthony rolled his eyes at the prince's stupidity.

"Fine, just do not wake me again. Only Aurora can do that," Cornelius said, and smiled. Anthony gagged at this comment and got off the seat. He heard movement from the trees and drew his sword. Something squawked and landed close to them. The creature turned its long neck and stared at them while they studied the strange beak and feathers. The bird then winked at them, and Anthony put his sword away. He remembered where he saw this beast before.

"Master Oryn?" Anthony said with confusion in his voice. It bowed its head and squawked again before disappearing into the woods.

"Ah, better," the men heard from the trees. Master Oryn appeared and smiled.

"Where the hell did you come from?" Cornelius sounded as arrogant as ever.

"Oh, just from following and capturing the little thorn in our side," Remus arrived at the camp with a limp body in his arms.

"Please, tell me he isn't dead!" Viviana said.

"He is quite alive, but you will not like who it is, Cornelius," Remus said and laid the body on the ground. The figure was that of a young man.

"He really was the most annoying one!" Cornelius growled when he saw the face of the assassin.

"Isn't that your youngest brother?" Aurora said, taking Cornelius' hand to provide comfort, but also keep him from slugging the unconscious brat.

"Yes, it is. That stupid, moronic, brainwashed monkey... Mother did this to him. He's not even old enough to woo a woman and here he is playing assassin," he said with malice in his voice. His mother's madness was like a disease that she spread to her husband and now her children.

"This is who you feared had escaped the mansion?" Anthony said to Remus, who shook his head yes.

"We will tie him up and interrogate him when he wakes. Once we question him..." Cornelius interrupted Viviana.

"We kill him?" He struggled to say the words.

"No! I will make a potion to wipe his memory and we leave him at the border. He will simply forget us and his mission. It worked for my attacker." Viviana saw Anthony cringe a little out of the corner of her eye. She knew he hated thinking about that night and what had happened.

"That sounds good, but we won't have much time. It's getting dark. We should wake him," Remus said and smiled. The young prince's body shook a little.

"Well, since we have little time... Get me a bucket of water!" Anthony readied to drench the assassin when he spoke.

"Do it and I will kill you," the young prince's eyes opened and stared at Anthony. He snarled his lips to look scary.

"Watch it, pup, or you will get knocked out again," Remus growled.

"You may have caught me off guard once… that will be the last time."

"You really are an idiot, aren't you, Octavius?" Cornelius hit him in the back of the head.

"My pathetic brother, you will suffer for your betrayal. I came to rescue you and now I see mother was right. You are with the enemy. I will kill you, along with Viviana." He looked at her with blood lust in his eyes. She allowed the anger she felt to rise, turning her eyes red and skin to glow with a pink hue. She watched the fear grow in the young man's eyes.

"You are only alive because of your blood. I burned you once and I can do it again. This time I will make sure you are ashes. How dare you come for me and think you can take my life. You need to be careful who you threaten. Now, answer their questions and I will spare you. If you choose not to cooperate, then I will make you pay!" She growled and then walked away from the group to calm down. She wanted to wring the life out of the pathetic boy but knew it would do nothing for them. She closed her eyes and breathed. When she opened them again, they had returned to their brilliant blue hue.

"What questions?" Octavius asked with panic in his voice. Anthony and Remus grilled him until the sun went down. Cornelius sat listening while the ladies made a fire and started dinner.

"He may be a well-trained assassin, but he sings like a lark," Viviana said in a low voice to Aurora.

"I think your little 'show' was quite effective in loosening his tongue. I know I would have been scared." Aurora shivered a little from the chill in the air, but Viviana wondered if she was a little scared of her, too.

"Sorry. It just seemed that he wouldn't sing unless he truly feared for his life. Plus, I'm a woman. We are scary when angered." She smiled at Aurora, who smiled back, but she could tell she was going to look at her differently now.

"I know you must have seen Cornelius use his powers before." Viviana was curious of Aurora's fear of her, since her husband had the same power.

"He has only set a lamp on fire once. When his temper flares, he becomes physically stronger, but nothing comparable to you and your abilities. Vi, you are unique. I have never heard of anyone being so powerful in their healing strength or their didymos."

"Didymos?"

"It's your second gift. Calestians who have special blood are born with two powers, usually healing and their didymos. Both abilities can be used for personal gain or to help others. That is pretty much all I know about it. They do not train Cornelius in either of his gifts. He has wanted to go to the Sun Shrine for ages, but his mother knew he did not have the heart for her evil plans, so she has kept him in the dark about it all."

"Well, I never knew what it was even called except my cursed side. I always just wanted to heal and help people, but the anger and the frustration I feel seems to boil my body and cause so much damage." She looked over at the men and remembered what she was going to do. "I should start the memory potion for the morning. It takes time to prepare properly, or I might wipe his mind completely blank." Viviana smiled but reminded herself that she would do no more harm to him unless he attacked her or her friends. Friends? She guessed she saw Aurora as more of a friend than just a traveler on the same journey. Viviana only had one or two girls as friends growing up because the boys fancied her and were always vying for her attention. It was nice to have a female, besides her cousin, to chat with and share her feelings. As she carefully filled the potion flask, she watched Aurora chatting with Cornelius and then looked at Anthony. She longed to talk to him alone and just be around him. Her heart started to beat faster as he approached her.

"Is the potion ready?" he asked, keeping an eye on the younger prince. Viviana sighed and pointed to the flask.

"It's ready. But we should wait until tomorrow morning so that way he will be out of it longer. It will take us some time to get him to the gate. So, what did he tell you?"

Cornelius answered that question. "Mostly about the assassination attempt of me and you. Also..." He hesitated.

"What?" Viviana didn't like the pause.

"He mentioned Great Aunt Gaiana."

"So?" Viviana knew nothing about this person.

"In my mother's twisted mind, she has the most powerful Calestius blood in the world. My mother believes that she can convince her to come to Dragoonus and be the leader of a monster army created by her."

"Monsters? Army? What are we talking about?" Aurora asked with fear in her voice.

"The men are being transfigured!" Anthony growled and cursed.

"Calm down, please! You knew about this?" Viviana pet his arm, trying to get him to focus on the conversation.

"It was a rumor, but I didn't dare believe it was real. That murderous, vile, treacherous woman…" Anthony was seething.

"She made me into this. It does not surprise me she is doing it to others. Queen Loviana needs this information now." Remus stroked his chin, thinking of a way to contact her.

"Thinking like that might hurt your brain, old friend. I think I am the solution to the problem." Master Oryn made Remus smile.

"What are you two planning?" Viviana was curious as well as scared.

"I will go ahead of the group and inform the queen about everything we have dealt with and found out from the little prince. Once informed, I will meet you all at the gate and take you safely to the Sun Shrine."

"But it's close to a three-day journey to the Shrine from the border. How will you get from here to there and back again before we are to the border? We will be there by tomorrow night or sooner." Oryn's plan confused Viviana.

"My dear girl, a magician never reveals his secrets!" He winked and with a flash of smoke, the old man was gone. Everyone stood in awe until Remus chuckled.

"That man always had a flair for a dramatic exit." He smiled and helped himself to a bowl of rabbit stew.

"Well, we need to all get some sleep before taking on the border patrol tomorrow. We will avoid the town by taking a side road Remus found and hopefully everything will go smoothly at the gate." Anthony looked around.

"Whatever we face tomorrow, we will meet it head on and get across to Calestius. There are no other options. I need help with my powers and Cornelius has vital information still for the Queen. We are both fugitives in our own homeland. Death is the only thing that can stop us. We have come this far and I, for one, want to see my next birthday in two days!" Viviana smiled. As long as they fought together, they would make it to face their fates.

"Aurora and I will take the first watch. You men look as if Death himself is hanging on your shoulders waiting for you," Viviana said while cleaning the dinner dishes. Anthony cleared his throat to say something, but stopped.

"I will rest in camp tonight and keep an ear out for the girls. They will be fine," Remus said, looking at Anthony.

"My lovely Aurora doesn't need protection. I will sleep like a baby, knowing my beautiful wife is guarding me." Cornelius squeezed her hand gently and gave her a kiss goodnight.

"Before I gag, would you two please go and get some sleep? I really don't need to suffer from such displays of emotion," Viviana said and smiled while rolling her eyes.

"Someone is just jealous!" Cornelius said jokingly.

"I wouldn't want anything like that from a man like you!" Viviana stuck her tongue out at him as the door shut.

"I think he is right, though," Aurora said sweetly to Viviana.

"Of course, I want a man to love me like he loves you. However, I have training for a potential war right now. I don't think love fits in my life at this moment," Viviana sighed and watched the fire dance. The flames seemed to rise and fall with her breathing. She never

171

noticed this before, and a thought crossed her mind. "Could I be more powerful than the 'most powerful' Calestian?"

"What are you thinking about, Vi?" Aurora asked and broke her from her internal conversation.

"I want this all to be over. No more hiding or watching and waiting for trouble. I need to get a good night's sleep."

"All of us do. We need more protection from that evil b… monster." Aurora corrected herself, and it made Viviana snicker.

"I'm just hopeful that my family is safe. If they can't get to me…" Viviana couldn't finish her sentence.

"Lord Bion is a smart and brave warrior. He will know how to protect all of his people." Aurora smiled and squeezed her hand. Viviana squeezed back and took a deep breath to center herself. She knew her feelings had to stay in check until they crossed the border, or she would endanger them all if she did anything to draw attention to their location.

"I'm going to get a drink of water. Would you like some?" Viviana asked Aurora and Remus.

"No, thank you," Remus said with his eyes closed. "You might check on the captive. Show him some charity and maybe erase his memory now."

"I'll come help you," Aurora offered.

"Thank you. Your presence should keep me from boiling the young prince from the inside out," Viviana looked towards the prince, sitting by the tabergo. She clenched her fists as they got closer to the young prince. He was wrestling with his restraints as they passed by and spat at them. The ladies just ignored him as they went to the water jug to get a drink. His eyes followed the cup as it raised and lowered from the women's lips.

172

"You look like you could use something to drink." Aurora offered him the cup.

"I'm sure you poisoned it, just like my brother!"

"So, you truly want a brutal and bloody war between Dragoonus and Calestius? Both types of blood run through your veins." Viviana spat the words at him. He tucked his head as if she struck him.

"These two bloodlines belong under one ruler. My mother and father want what is best for all these people," he said smugly.

"Your mother has completely brainwashed you. Your world will be different when your dear mother and father are removed by the very people you 'rule' over. War is coming and I'm afraid you are on the wrong side," Viviana said, and looked away from him. She felt the heat rising in her hands and she had to calm down.

"I think you should drink some water and sleep before we get to the border." Aurora looked deeply into Octavius' eyes, and he drank from the cup until it was empty. His eyes fluttered, and he passed out.

"Is he supposed to do that?" Aurora sounded worried.

"Yes, he will be out for the rest of tonight and tomorrow. The drug needs time to work and erase his memories." Viviana yawned and saw the stars slowly fading as they walked back to the fire.

"Do you want to wake the boys?" Aurora asked and yawned, too.

"No, give them time for a good sleep. We are going to need their strength if anything goes wrong tomorrow, or is it today?" Viviana looked and saw the darkness losing the sky to the light. Morning would come soon and bring with it another day filled with danger. She hoped for calmer days when they finally reached the Sun Shrine. They sat by the fire and waited for daybreak.

Chapter 22

The sun barely kissed the horizon when the boys opened the doors.

"Why didn't you two wake us earlier?" Anthony saw the bags under the girls' eyes.

"We knew you both needed sleep and the ride to the border was uneventful…" Aurora interrupted Viviana.

"We would have woken you if we needed you two to protect us…"

"You know I will do whatever it takes to keep you safe, my love!" Cornelius' cheesy line made everyone gag, even Aurora.

"Thank you, my hero. Now stop making everyone ill." Aurora put her hand over his scruffy lips. "Once we are in civilization again, you are shaving! You both look like beggars."

"Or like Remus," Viviana said and giggled. They all looked at Remus and he smiled wide, showing all his monstrous teeth. They all laughed and then the ladies yawned.

"And now it's time for sleep, girls. The boys can make their own breakfast." Remus eyed Viviana.

"But…" she was cut off by Anthony.

"Bed." He pointed to the tabergo, and the ladies moved that way, but Viviana stopped. She saw the sleeping young prince and checked his pulse. It was steady.

"He is fine until we get close to the gate. Someone will need to sneak him to a pub or a home somewhere to be found. We can't leave him out in the woods," Viviana said.

"Well, we could leave him, but it wouldn't be right." Aurora shrugged.

"Eh, I really don't care about right and wrong. I just care about him forgetting all of this." Cornelius made everyone realize that this young and brainwashed prince could cause a ruckus if he woke up before they passed the gate.

"Let's get him into the tabergo," Viviana said, and Aurora cringed. "I know, I know, but where else can we put him?"

"I will take him to the village ahead of you and leave him at the closest house I find." Remus scooped up Octavius' limp body. "The sooner we are rid of him, the better."

Everyone   and Remus disappeared into the woods. The rest of them readied for the rest of the trip.

"I just want to sleep." Viviana lay down and sighed.

"I am tired, too, but my mind is racing. Are you sure the potion worked on Octavius?" Aurora looked at Viviana, who was staring at the ceiling.

"I hope so. It is out of our hands," she said as she yawned and closed her eyes. "Sleep, Aurora."

"I will try." Aurora turned over and let the sound of the rolling tabergo lull her to dreamland.

As the day progressed, clouds moved in and blocked the sunshine. The wind picked up and whipped the orange and red leaves around the tabergo. When the road evened out, the horses quickened their pace. The wheels squeaked as they picked up speed. The trees thinned out and Anthony, with Cornelius by his side, could see the gate that would lead them to freedom from Dragoonus.

"We are close. Are you ready?" Anthony asked Cornelius, who started to breathe hard. "Do not get scared now! I need you to be a man; your wife needs you to be a man!"

"You are right. Let me get the papers in order and then we can go." He shuffled through a folder of papers he carried.

"Can you ask Vi to get me our papers?" Anthony asked Cornelius. The window opened and Aurora handed them some paperwork.

"Here they are. You two will be fine. Besides, if you need a woman to help with persuasion…" Aurora winked. Cornelius shook his head and furrowed his brow. She just rolled her eyes and shut the front window.

"Don't be mean to her. She is right. Sometimes it helps to have a beautiful woman by you," Viviana scolded from the window.

"Oh, hush you! I merely didn't like the idea of my wife using her womanly charm on other men."

"Jealous much?" Anthony asked jokingly.

"Time to be serious. We are at the gate," Cornelius said, trying to sound calm and in control, but his voice was shaking.

"Stop the carriage!" a guard ordered with annoyance in his voice.

"Hello," Anthony said with a charming smile. The guard eyed him intensely and held out his hand for the papers.

"All seems to be in order. May we see the female passengers?"

"Ladies, please join us," Cornelius said sweetly. Aurora and Viviana opened the doors and walked to the front of the tabergo.

"How may we help you, gentlemen?" Viviana asked, and smiled. The guards were thrilled to see such beauties, but then they frowned.

"We are looking for a woman who is very dangerous. Her name is Viviana, and it is said that she is traveling with a knight. Sir," a guard pointed to Anthony, "please raise your sleeve." Cornelius' and Aurora's eyes grew wide. They were done for!

"Of course." He showed them the handprint on his arm.

"What is that?" One guard asked, puzzled.

"Some say it is the handprint of an angel, and others say that I got into a brawl with a very hot-tempered woman one night. I was so drunk I really don't know which one is true." Anthony smiled, and the men laughed.

"Damn women! Oh, sorry ladies. No offense," the head guard said. "Well, everything looks fine to… what the hell?" The guard saw something climbing the wall by the trees.

"Get it, men!" They pointed crossbows at the wall.

"No," Viviana's right hand shot out towards the guards.

"Ahhhh, I'm on fire," one man said as he dropped to his knees.

"Get her!" the other guard pointed at Viviana.

"Go!" Anthony yelled as he fought off a guard. She sprinted off towards the gate but was tackled by a beastly looking man.

"Got you!" The guard grabbed her around the waist and then pulled her hair, which made her eyes tear up.

"Vi," Aurora said and then covered her mouth in horror after realizing what she had said.

"So, you are the witch we have been waiting for. They will handsomely reward me for your capture. Now do something. I bet you can't," he said, breathing heavily on her.

"I don't have to do anything. Aurora, I think this man is on fire, don't you?" Viviana motioned to the man.

"Look at me," Aurora said seductively. He looked, and she smiled. "You are on fire! You're burning!" she said, and the man started screaming in pain. He let go of Viviana and they turned from him.

"Put me out!" he screamed at them.

"With pleasure," Viviana kicked him in the groin, and it dropped him to his knees. She then used the shaft of the sword to knock him out completely.

"I had a feeling you were an incantatrix when you got Octavius to drink the potion," Viviana said, as Aurora bit her lip. "We should…" Viviana stopped mid-sentence to watch a man fly through the air and land upside down at the bottom of a tree with a thud. An inhuman growl from Remus scared many of the remaining guards into fleeing into the town for their lives.

She saw Anthony locked in battle with the head guard. The swords sang as they met over and over. Weaving in and out of the trees, the deadly dance went on until the guard attempted to remove Anthony's head and missed.

"Enough!" he yelled as he plunged the sword into the man's heart. With an animalistic cry, Anthony dropped to his knees, covered in sweat and blood. Viviana ran over and draped her arms around him. He gave her a half-hearted smile.

"Is that all of them?" he asked as Viviana helped him to his feet. Retrieving his sword from the guard's dead body, he cleaned it off and placed it back in its sheath.

"Yes. I am so sorry for all of this. I thought everyone was distracted," Remus said.

"It's done. I'm sure they would have tried something. I didn't trust that head guard." He put his hand on his mentor's arm.

"If we are ready, then let's get across before they regroup. I am done with this country!" Cornelius exclaimed. He pulled Aurora into his arms.

"Are you alright, my love?"

"Yes," she said and smiled at Viviana, "because of Vi. We make a great team."

"I am glad. Now let's go home and meet your family. Hopefully they like me."

"I'm sure you will charm them, just like you charmed me." Aurora kissed him sweetly.

"Get the tabergo across. The horses are a little spooked from the fighting." Anthony grabbed the reins and guided them to the Calestius side of the border. Two of Queen Loviana's guards waited on the other side to greet him.

"Come on everyone, our guides are here to assist us." Cornelius said. Then they all heard the gate swiftly close.

"What the hell?" Anthony shouted as he saw Remus shove Viviana out of the way before the gate came down

179

on her. He, however, was trapped on the Dragoonus side of the gate.

"NO!" Anthony shouted as he witnessed Octavius plunge a sword into the back of his friend. Viviana screamed, as if he had stabbed her as well.

"Brother, you will escort that whore back to this side of the gate, and I will not kill this miserable beast. Mother will deal with the two of you!" He spat the words at him with such venom and hatred that Cornelius cringed.

"Fine, leave the beast be and I will come to you, little brother," Cornelius said as he watched from the corner of his eye Viviana's transformation. He could feel the heat radiating from her and see the smoke rising from her fingers.

"LET... HIM... GO!" she shouted as the sound of sizzling and crackling filled the air. The metal gate danced and bend like noodles in a pot of boiling water. Droplets of the liquefied gate fell like scorching rain. The entire thing disintegrated in a matter of moments, and then the screaming started. Metal swords, helmets, and garb sang with the same sizzling sound as the gate. The Dragoonian guards ran hysterically towards town, leaving Octavius alone and a prime target for her wrath. She looked into his eyes, and he grabbed his head. They could see the smoke rising from his hair.

"ENOUGH!" Remus yelled and Viviana looked at him. His pained expression was for her. Hot tears flowed from her eyes, and she reached for him. "It will be fine, my lady. Let go!" And with those words, she fainted into the arms of Anthony. He held her as Cornelius and Aurora helped Remus back across the gate. The Calestian guards waited there with a cot for them to lay him on.

"We can't travel like this with him so badly hurt. What are we going to do?"

"You can find me a safe cave and leave me. I will heal in a few days, and I will come to the Shrine."

"Or Viviana can heal you. Get the salve from her bag, Aurora." Anthony laid Viviana down on his coat and rested her head gently on the ground.

"We have to go now before more Dragoonian guards come this way. The queen is waiting for us," Cornelius said as he looked towards the puddles of metal on the ground. "Nothing stands between us and them now."

"I have to heal him. She would never forgive me if I did not. Her blood is magical and will do the trick in no time," he said as he put the salve on Remus's wound. He then poked Viviana's finger for a few drops of blood and added them to a flask with water. He made Remus drink it and in a matter of moments, Remus' wound was gone.

"Astonishing," Aurora said as Remus got to his feet.

"I knew she was powerful, but I feel better than when we started the journey. I almost feel human." He smiled and everyone chuckled.

"We should go now. I hear rumbling, and it's not from the sky," Cornelius said, pointing towards town.

"We must move Lady Viviana and her company swiftly to the next town. The second platoon will wait here and protect the gate. If just one Dragoonian soldier comes across, you have my permission to arrest them. If they attack you, you defend yourselves," the head Calestian guard said.

"Wait for me!" Master Oryn appeared from the woods. The queen's guards drew their swords.

"Put those away, please. He is a part of our group. This is Master Oryn," Anthony said.

"We did not recognize you. Queen Loviana said you would accompany us. Please forgive us." The guards bowed deeply.

"It's not your fault that you suspected me. I have many faces and forms around the castle. Only her Majesty knows my true identity." He winked and rubbed his hands together. "So where is our sweet little girl who caused so much damage?" He surveyed the gate.

"She is in the tabergo. She probably will rest until we get to Calestius," Anthony said with a mixture of sadness and anger in his voice.

"We need to leave now," Cornelius heard the roar of soldiers coming towards them.

"Go," Anthony gave the orders to the horses, and they took off, almost throwing him from his seat. They all could hear men yelling behind them grow fainter as they moved down the road to Calestius' Sun Shrine.

Chapter 23

Close to sundown, the guards called for the group to rest at the inn in the town of Piaonius. The small but comfortable dining room held all of them, including Remus. The bar maid was shocked to see such a creature, but his polite and sweet manner charmed her. He enjoyed the company of people since it had been a long time in the woods, with only the occasional visits from the girls. His mind turned to his little one who lay in her bed, unconscious from the explosive display of her power. She saved his life. With all his heart, he wanted her to come enjoy the evening with them, but she was safer this way. He just had to keep watch over her; even with Anthony protecting her, she needed him.

"Remus, we should try to wake Viviana. She needs to eat and probably needs a bath before we leave tomorrow." Aurora's voice was filled with worry for Vi.

"Aren't we pressing on? Doesn't Vi need to be at the Sun Shrine before her birthday?" Cornelius asked the two.

"The queen told me she would be fine as long as we arrived at the Shrine before sundown on her birthday. She mentioned her full power would show itself at that time," the Calestian guard, Ioniaus, said between bites of food.

"What do you mean, full power?" Anthony asked as he choked on his ale.

"We are not sure, but I believe we will reach the Sun Shrine in the allotted time frame. If you will excuse me," Ioniaus said as he bowed and left the table.

"She's going to get worse. How in the world can she be contained? Her feelings drive her and she's a woman. No offense, my dear," Cornelius said, as he took a long drink from his cup.

"I have no idea what my queen has up her sleeve, but I trust her knowledge and understanding of our people. Great Aunt Gaiana, I believe, is much like Viviana. They have the same didymos," Aurora said as she placed her arm around her husband.

"Let's just hope she sleeps until we reach the Sun Shrine. Truthfully, I don't want to see her cause any more damage or hurt anyone else. She has enough guilt to deal with and I know any more will send her over the edge. She is strong, but so fragile too," Anthony said with a tender voice.

"You are right, Anthony. She needs all of us to keep her sane. I would hate for anger and sadness to rule her. Let us hope the queen knows what she is doing with our Vi." Remus drank the last of his ale and wiped his mouth.

"It's time to sleep. Anthony, take the first watch by Vi's door. I don't feel safe in this country yet. We are still too close to the border."

"You read my mind, Remus." Anthony headed up the stairs and took his post by Viviana's door. He opened the door to see her in the same position as he left her. Her slumber reminded him of a fairy tale his sister used to make him read, and he blushed. A kiss would not wake this fair maiden, who was no damsel in distress like in the story. He knew the curse she was under came not from any poisoned fruit or spell cast by an evil witch.

He sighed. Anthony wanted to lie next to her and watch her sleep, but instead, he closed the door and sat on the floor next to the room. Again, he felt responsible for her suffering. She would wake up and replay what she did over and over. He hoped that once they arrived at the Sun Shrine, the training would keep her mind busy and away from the horrors of the journey.

Hearing movement in the room, Anthony slowly inched the door open to see a black shadow with a pillow hovering over Viviana's face. He slid the door open just wide enough to sneak into the room. Watching the figure proceed to press the pillow down, Anthony leapt into the air and tackled the attacker.

They wrestled on the floor until Anthony pinned the man to the ground. He pulled the mask off and in the moonlight, he could see Octavius' face. Anthony growled. He applied pressure to the throat and waited for the struggling to stop. Octavius' body went limp, and Anthony relaxed for a moment, but then looked to the bed.

"Vi," he said as he removed the pillow from her face. She was breathing! He sighed in relief that he was not too late. She moved and opened her eyes. He spoke, but his words were cut short by a blade in his back. Anthony roared in pain.

"This is what you get for getting in my way," Octavius hissed in his ears. Anthony staggered from the bed and fell to the ground. Octavius smiled as he watched him gasp for air.

"Now I will…" His voice stopped as he looked down and saw a sword sticking out of his chest. Octavius stumbled to the ground and saw that Viviana was no longer in bed. His eyes searched for her, and he could see her standing in her gown that was swaying in the breeze from the open window.

"This time, I'll remove your head with my bare hands," she said as she moved towards the prince.

"Please, go get help, Vi!" Anthony gasped. She forgot about the prince and rushed to Anthony's side.

"The only help you need is mine," she said as she got down on her knees and slowly removed the blade. He grunted, trying not to cry out in pain. Placing her hand on the wound, she took the pain away and he could breathe with ease.

"Now save Octavius." Anthony sat up and saw the icy stare of death in the young prince's eyes. It was too late, but Viviana did not seem to care. He looked at her.

"You can only be attacked so many times… he needed to die." Viviana's cool tone made Anthony very nervous.

"Well, I guess it was only a matter of time before you finally came to your senses," Cornelius said from the doorway. "I heard a commotion but wasn't sure where it was coming from, or I would have been here faster. Looks like the guards from the queen are dead. That little bastard…" he trailed off when Aurora arrived at the door.

"So, I guess we weren't safe, even on Calestius soil. Is he finally dead?" She pointed to the body.

"I hope so. I'm exhausted after trying to kill him so many times. He is stronger than I could have imagined. His healing abilities were astonishing and quite annoying." Viviana sat on the bed and sighed. "I wonder if they would be kind enough to prepare a bath for me. I am covered in blood."

"I will go and see," Aurora said and quickly left the room.

"Thank you. I guess we should see about burying the bodies. They won't be left for the animals." She grabbed a sheet and draped it over the body.

"We will figure something out. You go take a bath and thank you again for saving my life." Anthony smiled, and even in the pale candlelight from the hall, he could see her blush.

"You saved me from being smothered, so I think it's only fair. Besides, Aunt Mathilda would make my life a nightmare if anything happened to her baby boy." She smiled as she touched his face. It was now his turn to blush. Viviana enjoyed the sight of her protector being a little embarrassed.

"They're drawing a bath now, Vi," Aurora said from the doorway.

"I'm coming," she said, and grabbed a robe from her closet. As she left, Anthony's eyes tracked her down the hall and he shuddered. Cornelius raised an eyebrow.

"Ah, so Aurora is right. You are into your cousin. *Is* she your cousin, or something else? You know more than you let on about her." He caught Anthony off guard, and it made him start to mumble.

"What are you saying?"

"There is something very special about Viviana, and our relationship with each other is not what everyone believes it is. I can't say anything more than this. She can't know..." He stopped.

"You can tell me. I won't tell anyone," Cornelius said, and Anthony believed him, but the secret had to stay that way until they reached the Sun Shrine.

187

"You will know when we reach our destination," Anthony said and then pointed to Cornelius's brother's body. "What do we do with him?"

"I have the guards buried, but he has to go back to the gate." Master Oryn appeared in the doorway. The boys jumped and cursed under their breath. Oryn was right, but that meant the body had to go somewhere for the rest of the night.

"So, where do we store him until morning?" Cornelius asked frankly. He felt no remorse for what happened to his flesh and blood.

"No need for that. Remus and I will take the body back tonight. No one must see what we are doing. The cover of night will cloak us as we move through the woods," Master Oryn said as he removed the body from the room. "The innkeeper will move Viviana to a room with no window and clean this one up before dawn. I want Anthony in the room with her. More guards from the castle will meet you at the next town, which is a day's ride from here. Please leave right before dawn to arrive on time. You know how important it is to get Viviana safely to the Shrine on time." Oryn emphasized the last sentence, and the boys left the room.

"You should find Aurora and get some sleep. I will find you when we need to leave." Anthony said..

"Try to get some sleep, too. You are a bear when you are sleep deprived," Cornelius said with a smile. Anthony smiled back.

"Just be ready to go," Anthony said and left to secure Viviana's room.

While waiting, he made sure he had a bed made up on the floor. She might have a problem with him there, but he had his orders.

188

"Oh, I see you are making yourself comfy." Viviana's honey-toned voice made Anthony jump. He turned to see her in a flowing red colored nightgown that hugged every womanly curve of her vivacious body.

"Remus thought…" She looked at him and he couldn't speak.

"He told me the plan before they left. I am feeling much safer sleeping with you," she paused and smiled, "in my room." He swallowed hard and just nodded. She had tried for so long to keep from distracting Anthony from his duty, but her longing to show him her feelings overwhelmed her senses. No longer caring about duty or honor, she saw this as a golden opportunity to express her feelings for him.

"You should sleep, Vi. Tomorrow we start before dawn." He would not look at her.

"That will be soon. Why try to sleep? There must be something better to do." The tone of her voice made him squirm.

"Sleep is the only thing to do." Anthony closed his eyes.

"Ah, so sleep, huh? I heard there are many more things that can happen in the dark of night, especially if two people want it."

"It is not appropriate at this time and besides, you are a lady…"

"Not a whore? Is that what you like?" Her voice made him look at her.

"Viviana! What has gotten into you?" he asked, with anger in his voice.

"I finally know what I want, and I don't care about the consequences. Why can't I be happy?" she snarled at him. Obviously, she wasn't tempting enough, not like Aurora. She would be happy once Anthony was out of her

189

hair and she could focus on other things. Love be damned!

"I am your protector. How would I protect you if we were…"

"I know. You're right. Please just forget everything I said. Goodnight," Viviana rolled over in her bed and quietly let the tears stream down her face. She let sleep whisk her away until morning.

Chapter 24

The warmth of the sun filled the room, and Viviana stirred. She tried to get out of bed, but her body was heavy. Her head hurt and she didn't want to get up, but a splash of cold water hit her face and made her jump.

"Adilynn!" Viviana opened her eyes to Aurora.

"Forgot my name?" She looked at her, puzzled.

"Sorry. My cousin used to do that to me. You remind me of her sometimes," Viviana said, getting out of bed.

"Oh, you mean Anthony's sister. I will take that as a compliment then," Aurora smiled, but noticed Viviana's eyes. "Were you crying?"

"No, I just woke up. I didn't sleep well." She tried to hide her face.

"Why? Did you and Anthony fight?"

"I made a fool of myself and probably hurt Anthony," she sighed, remembering what she said.

"It happens. I know it's not my place, but he cares deeply for you and doesn't want you to do anything you will regret later. Cornelius could resist me until we got

191

married," Aurora saw the blush on Viviana's face and knew her instincts were right.

"We… I mean me… I mean… how did you know?"

"You are in love with him. Don't deny it. Besides, I did the same thing with Cornelius. We believe that if a man really wants us, then they will be quite willing to warm our bed. The men who don't are the ones who love us the most. Worthless men have no problem taking a pretty girl to bed; the ones who respect you enough to resist their urges are worth their weight in gold. You are very lucky Anthony is in love with you."

"So, it's not because he is not attracted to me? Or because we are cousins?" Viviana wanted to believe her, but she just wasn't sure of Aurora's advice.

"He doesn't know what the future holds and if he took a precious gift like that from you and he died…" Viviana gasped at the thought.

"You are right, but it doesn't make it any easier. I still want him, and it's killing me. I feel so different after this attack. I'm burning inside, and Anthony's the only one who can cool me down." The look in her eyes was very familiar to Aurora.

"You better find something else for now. He won't give in anytime soon and I don't think you will get married…" Viviana stopped Aurora.

"Marriage?" she said and almost fell to the floor. Viviana wasn't even thinking about that, but Anthony is a knight and brought up to uphold a lady's honor. Marriage was the only way for them to occupy the same bed.

"So, you two never…"

"No, and I am pretty sure he has never been with any woman." Aurora smiled at Viviana's look of relief.

"I guess we should get downstairs to the boys. I see the sunlight creeping down the hallway." Viviana grabbed her bag, and the girls made their way to the stables.

"I was about ready to come in there and drag you two out here," Cornelius said jokingly, and smacked Aurora's butt. Before he could react, she swung around, grabbed his sword, and smacked him with the flat of the blade.

"Ouch!"

"Baby!" she said, laughing at him.

"Let's go. Viviana, would you sit with me, please?" Anthony offered his hand, and she took it.

"That means you and me in the back," Cornelius said with great enthusiasm and Aurora, and she groaned as they got in the tabergo. They started off out of town and Anthony's silence was killing Viviana.

"Anthony, I just want to say I'm sorry. I acted completely unladylike, and I am ashamed of myself."

"Vi, you have no reason to apologize. You have gone through so much and your head was not in the right place."

"No, it was in a fine place. I just know you are not the type of man who would take advantage of any woman, even if she showed you she was attracted to you. You are not interested in me that way, and I accept that." She was trying to goad him into talking and she saw it working. He sat chewing on his lip. Anthony opened his mouth to say something, but just grunted.

Viviana kept quiet while he gathered his thoughts, but she became anxious and fidgety. She saw a town and pointed it out to Anthony. He nodded and stopped.

"Please switch spots with Cornelius. We will be careful with you this time." He tried not to look into her eyes while speaking to her. She took this as a bad sign and moved to the inside without a word.

193

She felt like he had just stabbed her in the chest, and she wasn't sure why. He hadn't answered her about why he refused her advances, and then he sent her away from him. It all stung, and she had a horrible time trying to stifle her tears.

"Vi, what's wrong?" Aurora saw her wipe her eyes.

"I'm not sure, but Anthony said nothing about last night and then banished me. It hurts. I'm also furious." Viviana could feel the heat rising in her hands. She took deep breaths to calm down.

"I think he's not sure what to say. He obviously doesn't want to hurt you, but he might with whatever he says. Men have a horrible time expressing their feelings. Then when they do, they still end up saying the wrong thing. I'm sure when the time is right; he will try to explain everything to you."

"Honestly, I should just stop caring. He will go home after I am safely at the Sun Shrine. I don't need him impeding my training and I'm more powerful than him. He is of no use to me. If you could please, wake me when we arrive at the Shrine."

"I will. Get some rest," Aurora said.

"Sun Shrine… queen's guards… Viviana…" Aurora put her ear up to the door near the men and tried to hear more, but she fell to the ground when they stopped abruptly.

"Ouch," she said quietly and got to her feet. She opened the window and saw eight guards standing in front of them. Their armor glistened in the sunlight, blinding all who looked at them. One of the guards came forward and gestured to the tabergo.

"I'm guessing the treasure is secured on board the carriage?" he said with a smile. His mustache moved like a caterpillar on his lip. His olive-green eyes, dark

194

complexion, and hints of white hair around his face gave him an air of authority.

"And you are?" Anthony eyed the man suspiciously as he put his hand on the top of his sword.

"No need for that, lad. As you can see by the crest on my shield and colors I fly, I am a member of the elite royal guard. Orville is my name, and you must be Anthony and the young prince, Cornelius. You have grown since we last met." He smiled momentarily and then became quite serious. "We must move swiftly to get the lady to her destination. Time is our enemy, and the queen does not know what peril we will face if she is not there by sundown tomorrow. We should ride on horseback. My men will take a passenger until nightfall. Then we will switch for the second leg of the journey."

"Um, Viviana's asleep and probably should stay that way until we get the Shrine," Aurora said, and Orville grunted.

"Switch out horses with fresh ones and we will try to ride through until tomorrow. We will have to come back for our horses later," Anthony said. Cornelius saw the look on Anthony's face and helped.

"Anthony, Aurora and I can stay behind. Go to the Shrine. We will give the horses' time to rest and join you in a day or so." He looked at Aurora and she smiled.

"Are you afraid of Viviana?" Anthony asked them. They both looked at the ground. "I don't blame you since I am too. Besides, Viviana and I would appreciate having our horses."

"We will leave tomorrow before noon and be there in less than a day. That should give the horses enough time to rest." Cornelius got down.

"Over there we can purchase fresh horses," Orville said and pointed to a small thatched roofed dwelling, with smoke rising from the chimney, close to the edge of town.

"Get what you need while I unhook the horses. When everyone is rested, get to the Shrine as soon as possible. Aurora, I think Viviana's going to need you. I know you are not Adilynn but…"

"She has adopted me; I guess you could say. There is much she is going to deal with when she arrives at the Sun Shrine, isn't there Anthony?" she asked, looking in his eyes.

"Yes, and she may never forgive me for it." He looked down at the ground and rubbed his forehead.

"Wha… never mind. Just stay safe. We will see you in a few days." Aurora hugged Anthony, and he quickly hugged her back and moved away from her. "And Viviana is going to need you more than ever. Her power is linked to her emotions. Do not let her wall up her heart, especially from you. Make her forgive you for whatever you have been keeping from her," she whispered to him. He nodded.

"Stay safe," Anthony said and got on the tabergo.

"Let's go!" Orville ordered, and the caravan started on the last leg of the journey. The guards flanked the sides of the tabergo to protect it from any type of attack.

As they continued down the road, they were closer to the Sun Shrine. Signs welcoming travelers appeared on posts and towns grew more populated. Anthony tried to keep his eyes open, but the warm air and rhythmic movement of the ride made his eyelids feel like lead.

"You know you can rest. We can drive the tabergo. You are safe with us," Orville said with a warm smile on his face.

"I should, but I still don't feel safe. After everything that has happened…"

"I know. Master Oryn informed us of all the ordeals you have endured on this voyage. I give you my word as a gentleman and a knight that I will protect you and your charge. Nothing will harm either of you. Please let me take the reins." Orville slid off his horse and jumped up to the seat by Anthony.

"If I may, I will sleep here. I am not comfortable in confined spaces." Anthony moved and yawned loudly.

"As you wish, lad." The leader commanded the knights to continue.

The night moved swiftly as the well-guarded carriage flew over the road. They made an impressive time. When they stopped to rest, they were only halfway to their destination. The horses whinnied as they ate their food, and the smell of cooking woke Anthony from his deep slumber.

"Here is some food. You looked starved. We are less than half a day's ride from the Shrine, but they needed a quick rest for all. I hope you slept well." Orville smiled at Anthony's full mouth grin.

"Thank you for everything so far, Master Orville," Anthony said between bites of warm oatmeal and berries.

As he finished his meal, he thought about seeing Queen Loviana again. He was just a child when they first met, but she made quite an impression on him. She personally healed him after a brutal beating by one of the older boys. He tried his hardest not to cry, but his eyes burned from holding them back and he couldn't hide it any longer.

"This is not a sign of weakness, sweet boy. Pain is inevitable, but what we do with it is our own choice. Harness your feelings and channel them into the power to protect the ones you love. That makes the greatest knight of all." She kissed his forehead, and all the pain was gone. He bowed deeply to her and left the infirmary to join his classmates again. She was a large part of why he became an elite knight. He wanted to protect her, but never had the chance. Anthony wondered if she would remember him at all.

"Time to move!" Orville's voice brought him back to the present. The tabergo started moving, and he focused on the task at hand. Viviana would need to wake once they got her to the Shrine. He did not like the idea of being the one to wake her, since he feared what she might do to him. After their last conversation, he knew she was not happy with him.

Watching the sun move in the sky, Anthony almost missed the fact that the Shrine was right in front of them. His eyes widened as he took in the immense size of the temple. The arches and high-pitched roof looked more like a school of learning than worship. Crops and cattle filled the land around them, and the homes of the farmers and ranchers looking much nicer than Anthony had ever seen for peasants.

He gulped as he passed through the gates of the massive building. The structure was much grander than it appeared from the outside. The dome shaped Sun Shrine sparkled in the light like a golden beacon. Surrounding the actual temple were several buildings connected by walkways and decorated with columns of art. Each painting had vibrant colored scenes of history. Anthony recognized some of the pictures from his training. Of course, they depicted the stories differently than what he learned in school. He realized just how much the Dragoonus Council twisted history.

As he stared at a picture of a beautiful girl being chased by a man with a sword in hand, he heard a scream from the tabergo. Jumping off his seat, Anthony swiftly moved to the back of the tabergo and was smacked in the face as the door swung open. Viviana ran from the open door screaming like a mad woman possessed by pain and despair. Anthony took off after her but could not catch up to her. He tripped over a small rock and took a fall in the grass. As he lay in pain, he saw a man appear from thin air. He wrapped her in his arms and carried her to a fountain, where the statue of a mystical nymph poured a constant stream of icy mountain water into a marble pool.

"NO!" she cried as he dunked her under the water.

"Get your hands…" the sight of Queen Loviana silenced Anthony.

"He is doing what I asked, Anthony."

"Theron would not hurt our beloved Viviana." Her honey-sweet voice calmed him, but then he felt very confused.

"Theron?" Anthony looked from the water to the queen.

"You call him Remus. He is human… well, mostly human, again." She pointed to the fountain, and he saw steam rising from the ice-cold water. He could also see the burns on Remus's face and paws. All Anthony could do was sit there and wait for Viviana.

"Come with me, Theron. I will help you with your wounds. It will take a few more minutes for her to cool down." Queen Loviana smiled at him, and he left Viviana in the water.

As the queen tended to Remus, Anthony watched the steam slowly disappear. The queen gracefully walked over to the pool and stared into the water. Her eyes met Viviana and Viviana gasped. She raised her head from the water and stared. It was like seeing a reflection of an older self. The sapphire eyes and the silky auburn hair were identical to hers. Their noses were slightly off, and Viviana had bigger cheeks, but this woman looked just too much like her.

Viviana rose from the water and her legs felt like jelly. She collapsed into this woman's arms. Viviana felt a jolt and triggered a memory.

"Who are you?" she whispered as her eyes welled with tears.

"You will know soon enough, but now you need to rest," Queen Loviana said, and Viviana closed her eyes.

"My lady, the room is ready for her." A young man, in a servant's uniform, bowed his head.

"Thank you, Sacarius. Anthony, please take our rose to her room. Hopefully, she will sleep for the next few hours."

"But the feast? She hasn't eaten in almost two days," Remus, now Theron, said with concern in his voice.

"You are right. I will come to the room in an hour and see if she can go. She will have many questions." Queen Loviana transferred Viviana's limp body into Anthony's arms. She stroked her wet hair and motioned to the servant. "Please escort them to the living quarters."

"Yes, my queen." He bowed and then looked at Anthony. "This way, sir."

Passing many closed doors covered in intricate designs, they made their way to Viviana's room.

"Where are we?" she whispered into his ear. He stumbled for a moment and then composed himself again.

"The Sun Shrine. We are here in your room. I thought you were asleep," he whispered back.

"I was pretending because I felt something so intense... I just passed out for a moment."

"Well, stay still and I will explain everything when we get into the room," he said, and she adjusted her head against Anthony's shoulder. Opening the door, the servant motioned for Anthony to stay at the door.

"The door on the left is the bathing room and the one on the right is to the sleeping chambers. Please remove your shoes before going in."

Anthony nodded, and the servant left him and Viviana alone.

"You can put me down now, please." She tried to get down out of his arms.

"I will, but in bed. You don't need to tire yourself out any more than you have." Anthony kept a firm grip on her as he removed his shoes and moved to her bedroom.

"Okay, now tell me what happened!" She was getting impatient.

"Fine, but you are not going to like it." He knew this time would come, but he never wanted to tell her like this.

"Oh," she said, quite taken aback by his statement. "Well, just tell me what happened when I got here. How did I get in the water?" She shivered and wrapped the blankets around her.

"First, you should get some dry clothes on, Lady Viviana," Queen Loviana's voice came from the doorway.

"Your Majesty." Anthony rose and bowed.

"You are off the hook from your duties for now. I need time with her to explain everything. There is so much to tell you." She looked to Viviana, who sat in awe of the queen. She then looked at Anthony who left.

"Your shoes, Anthony." Viviana smiled and pointed to the other room.

"Thank, Vi," he said and left.

After shutting the door, the queen motioned for her to go to the closet, where they picked up a golden dress with a trim of blue that reminded Viviana of the sky before the sun set. The sleeves sat loosely on her shoulders, while the neckline displayed the tops of her breasts. The queen helped her dry her hair by the warm fire and brushed it gently for her.

During this time, they talked about Viviana's life. She talked about her mother, Ambrosiana, and Lord Bion. They discussed time at the University and her philosophy on several subjects. Viviana enjoyed their time talking, but was still not fully sure about what was going on and what happened when they arrived.

"I do not wish to be rude, your majesty, but I must ask what happened to me?" Viviana hoped not to offend her hostess.

"Please call me Lovie when we are in private." She smiled as Viviana nodded. "Now, feel the back of your neck."

Viviana did and gasped. She looked scared. "My birthmark is raised, and it's red hot, but it doesn't feel like it's burning me."

"The mark is your source of power. Each person who possesses power has a mark. Mine is on my foot." She took off her shoe, and she had a rose in full bloom, with one petal missing.

"So, a rose is a symbol everyone has?"

"No. Each bloodline has a unique symbol." The queen waited for Viviana to understand what she had just said.

"We… are… related?" Viviana said hesitantly.

"Yes. I think you have noticed how we look very similar." She watched as Viviana's eyes widened and filled with tears.

"How is this possible? Are you my mother's sister or cousin or…" Viviana tried to think of every option but stopped.

"You are my daughter, Viviana. You are the dead princess. I gave you to Ambrosiana to take care of and faked your death."

"What?" she backed up from the queen. The room started to spin, and she couldn't breathe.

"I'm so sorry, my princess. I had to leave you, but I did with such wonderful people. They helped you become such a stunning young woman."

"You can't be my mother. My mother is dead…" She tried not to faint from the news. Tears rolled down her cheeks as she sat down on the couch. "Please, just leave me alone."

"As you wish, Viviana, but I will return when it is time for the feast." Queen Loviana left the room, leaving Viviana trying to deal with her new identity.

As she lay there on the couch, she continued to cry. Nothing made sense anymore,, and she just wanted to see her father. *But if what the queen said is true, then he isn't my father. He had been lying to me all this time.* The feelings of betrayal and anger bubbled up, and the tears flowed until she fell into a dreamless sleep.

Chapter 25

"Damn it!" Viviana awoke to a throbbing pain. She placed her hand on her symbol, on her neck, and took deep breaths until it was gone. Looking around the room, she could see the daylight disappearing on the horizon. "I hate this. Now, not only am I a fire starter, but I am also a dead princess."

As she moved into the living room, she looked out the window overlooking a beautiful garden. Her neck felt better, but the pain in her heart still lingered. "Why, mother? Why couldn't you prepare me for this? You should have told me!" she said out loud and turned to see Queen Loviana sitting on the sofa.

"I see you are awake. I wanted to let Ambrosiana tell you, but I knew the truth would only cause this pain. I didn't believe you could handle it until you were older." The queen sat still as she watched Viviana's reaction.

"I understand it was for my protection, but that means everyone in my life has lied to me." Viviana thought of her mother and father. "Even… Anthony?" It sucked the air out of her lungs as if she was punched in the gut. Tears appeared in her eyes as she shook with a thousand emotions. "He knew! He knew this whole time!" she shouted, and it felt like a thousand tiny knives stabbed her in the heart.

"Your majesty, they are ready for…" Anthony saw the look on Viviana's face, and he braced for the worst.

"You!" She ran at him and hit him with all her might. "You knew!" she cried and ran from the room. He watched her running down the hall and just stood there.

"I…" he tried to speak, but nothing came from his lips. He looked at the queen, who rose from the sofa and came to his side.

"Go after her. She needs you and you need her." She placed her hand on his shoulder.

"She will never forgive me for this," he said as a single tear rolled down his newly shaven face.

"You won't know unless you go after her. She is in pain, but she also understands why we did what we had to do. Viviana may not forgive you right away, but she will soon. Her heart aches to be loved and to love you." The queen smiled, and Anthony bowed. He walked swiftly from the room and headed after Viviana.

Losing the light of day, Anthony searched the grounds until he found Viviana in the barn. He climbed up to the hayloft and made his way slowly to the corner where she was laying. Her body shook with each sob, and he, too, cried.

"I'm so sorry, Vi." The tears rolled down his cheek and caught her off guard.

"You lied to me! You are a horrible, horrible person. You're not my cousin, not even by marriage. Oh, and Adilynn, how could you?" Viviana cried out in anger in

205

between sobs. He tried to hold her, but she slugged his arm as hard as she could, and Anthony flinched in pain.

"What do you have to say for yourself?" she asked, looking into his eyes.

"Damn it, woman! What do you want from me? Your father placed me in the royal guard as a child because he said one day I would protect the most precious treasure in the land. I didn't know about you until much later and your father swore me to secrecy. It's not my fault that I fell in love with you, and it tortured me every day that I couldn't tell you the truth. You had to deal with so much…"

"I know in my head that everything you say is true, but it still hurts. How can I trust you? How can I trust anyone? I really don't like you right now." She tried to keep herself calm, but her anger was rising, and her hands trembled.

"I can handle that, but it doesn't keep me from protecting and loving you…" He stopped when she turned to him, looking stunned.

"You said you love me." It hit her like a brick when he said the words again. She wiped her eyes as he put his hand on her check, but Viviana pushed him away. "You can't just say the words, and everything will be fine. I'm so confused." He moved close to her, and she blushed when he pulled her into his arms. Gently he put his lips on hers. She became limp in his arms, and he tried to stifle a grin.

"What's so funny?" She thought he was laughing at her and it made her stiffen her whole body.

"Relax, relax." He held her tighter as she tried to wiggle out of grasp. "Hey, I wasn't laughing at you. Please," he said sweetly, and she stopped struggling. "I've never had a woman become putty in my arms. You just melted." He wrapped his arms around her tighter, gave her a kiss on the forehead. She rested her head against his chest and heard his steady heartbeat. This calmed her head and her heart. All the tension between them was gone.

"I really don't like you," she said as she hugged him tightly.

"I know I cannot apologize enough..." Anthony kissed her auburn hair gently.

"No, it's just I can't be mad at you. You have such a calming effect on me, and even when I want to dislike you, it never lasts very long." She picked up her head and looked into his eyes. "I'm sorry, Anthony. You are not to blame, nor is anyone else. It's just so much to grasp. My father..." Tears flowed again.

"He's a great man who gave you a safe and peaceful life. Lord Bion may not be your blood kin, but he has done everything for you that a father is expected to do for their child. He loves you like no other person can, and you know that."

"You are right. He and my mother gave me everything I needed to get to this place." She hugged him harder. "I'm just so scared. I'm just a lord's daughter. I am not cut out for being a princess, let alone a queen. Let's also not forget that I have an extremely volatile didymos that could lead to massive destruction. I need a few decades to deal with all of this insanity." Viviana took a breath and let out a frustrated scream.

"Feel better?" Anthony rubbed his ears.

"Sorry. Oh, and I guess I should tell you; I love you too!" She smiled, wrapped her arms around his neck and kissed him deeply.

"I know. You sometimes talk in your sleep," he said with a smirk and dodged her fist.

"You are horrible." She scrunched her nose at him and ran off to the Sun Shrine, with Anthony trying to catch her the entire way.

By the time they made it back to the ballroom, the feast had begun. The room smelled of fresh bread and mead, which made Viviana's stomach growl. Anthony nabbed a tart from a server and handed it to her. She smiled, grateful for his thoughtfulness. They watched the festivities until a girl in her early teens approached them.

"Lady Viviana, Her Majesty, requests you to return to your room so you may freshen up before eating." The girl seemed to keep her distance and made Viviana feel a little awkward.

"Yes, of course. If you will excuse me, Anthony," she said and squeezed his hand.

"I will tell the others," he whispered to her and let her hand go. She wanted Cornelius and Aurora to know before anything else happened. Viviana left with the standoffish girl, headed back to her room, and hoped the others would take the news better than she did.

She forgot everything when she saw all the women dressed like celestial beings. Feeling more common and out-of-place as they traveled through the halls, she tried to hide her eyes from everyone and walk close to the wall.

"Everyone who was anyone in Calestius was at the Sun Shrine for the Moon Festival, which illuminates the courtyard and said to be a significant source of healing." Viviana stopped listening to the girl when they reached her room.

"Thank you, Evie. I will help Viviana for now." Queen Loviana dismissed her with a wave of her hand, but with a warm smile.

"You were really nice to that girl. She was quite snotty to me, but I do smell a bit, I guess." Viviana tried to straighten her hair and brush some hay from her dress.

"I have not introduced you yet to the others, so most of the royalty here will be that way. Oh, and that is your cousin from my sister Faiana. She is a dear friend to me, so I put up with her 'snotty' children." She giggled. "I don't think I have had anyone described them like that."

"Well, I have dealt with enough privileged children and most of them really are like that."

"And you?"

"People are people. Rich or poor. Everyone has value and has the right to live a fruitful life. I do not feel sorry for a farmer's daughter because I have seen them at the University. They learn and joke and live just like anyone with some money in their pockets. We only limit ourselves by not fighting for what we believe is right. A noble, a farmer, and a merchant can all sit at a table and eat together as if they were brothers. Our status should not dictate how we succeed in life." Viviana realized she was rattling on and paused. She looked embarrassed.

"There is no shame in your passion, my sweet girl," Queen Loviana said with a smile. "In fact, you will need it for running the country. People will pull you in many directions and you need that passion to stand up for your beliefs."

"This is making me more and more nervous."

"You are my child, and you will rise to this challenge as you have in the past. You would not be here without the strength you have burning inside of you."

"How am I your child? What is the story that no one has ever told me?"

"I had to give you to Ambrosiana and claim you as dead to keep you safe. I had a niece, your age, here that

209

passed away from a horrible fall. We used her death as yours." The queen's eyes filled with tears, and she had to stop to compose herself. "I told her to keep you hid away until you were older and could accept your role as Auriana Cleopatra Viviana, princess of Dragoonus," she said and motioned for Viviana to sit down by her.

"She told me when I was little that I was a secret love child between Lord Bion and herself. She said that she was bound to your side and so she kept my existence secret from Lord Bion until you released her when you left. She said you tried to make her go to him, but she was ashamed of herself. Then, when you left, she had nowhere to go and had to let Lord Bion know of me. He was still in love with her and so they wed in a small chapel, which made her the mistress of the Manor and me his legitimate child. Mother used to tell me about a little girl I used to play with, and I always guessed it was the dead princess." Viviana remembered the stories vividly.

"Well, Ambrosiana loved your father for years, and I guess the feelings became mutual." The queen smiled.

"Oh, yes. Father adored my mother... Sorry." She saw Queen Loviana's eyes saddened when she used the word 'mother.'

"No need, Viviana. I may have given birth to you, but your mother raised you." The tears came back, and Viviana put her arm around her. The warmth and smell of the queen made her feel comfortable, like coming home. Fragments of memories surfaced again, and Viviana's eyes filled with tears too. Mother. The word whirled around in her head like the wind through branches. The thought of having another mother made her happy, but angry at the same time. The feeling of abandonment from both Ambrosiana's death and the queen giving her up to save her made her sick to her stomach. She pulled away from the queen.

"Why couldn't you keep me safe here? Why did you give me away?" Viviana's question made her newly found mother stiffen.

"Your blood father, Demosthenes, had ordered our death. I was still considered a Calestian, but a child's kingdom was determined by their father and that made you a citizen of Dragoonus. Keeping you on Calestius ground would start a war, which Raphiana wanted. That's why she planted the idea of adultery in his head."

"I thought he became ill and went crazy."

"He was insane with jealousy. I loved the king very much. He was romantic and wooed me, even though we had an arranged marriage. However, before all of this had happened, I had become smitten with a young knight who also was wonderful at wooing women. Raphiana found out about my old flame and that's when everything went downhill. She used her powers to poison the king, and he became paranoid and controlling. Even with all the love we showed each other, nothing could save us." She paused and then touched Viviana's face. "You have his chin and his ears. I convinced him you were his until you were almost two. You looked much more like me. Raphiana did everything she knew to twist him into a crazed, paranoid, and jealous man who believed I had betrayed him. You were so sweet and beautiful as a child, but his love for you and me was just not strong enough. It is all my fault… I gave that lying, manipulative bitch the opportunity she needed." Queen Loviana sighed and rubbed the temples of her head.

"And I thought me being in love with my cousin was crazy." Viviana smiled, and the queen chuckled.

"Yes, family can be wonderful or a complete nightmare."

"So now what? Now that I know the insane truth about my past, what do I do with it?"

"Now you must train enough to make it to your Great Aunt Gaiana's land. She, hopefully, will give you the tools and wisdom to control your powers. I also need you to convince her to come and fight on our side once the war begins. Raphiana wants Gaiana to lead her army against us. When you take the throne–"

"What?" Viviana jumped up from the lounge chair. "Who said anything about me ruling the country?"

"Why do you think I kept you safe? I knew one day you would be ready to take your place as the heiress to the Dragoonus' throne. I hoped your father, the king, would have lived to see you, but I had a feeling that Raphiana would take care of him and use her husband as a puppet king. She has poisoned him like Demosthenes, so he is in no shape to control her. That vile woman will start her war and try to take over as much land as she can with her powers." She looked at Viviana and smiled. "She never factored you into her equation. We will keep your identity safe until your return from the dictum Vaille.

"I have never heard of that place." Viviana sounded worried.

"They also referred it to as the Eternal Nightfall Forest." The queen searched through the closest and retrieved a ruby colored dress, with lace trim. She helped Viviana dress and fix her hair. "You and Anthony will leave in three months."

"I don't know if that is enough time to control my powers or even be ready for another journey." Viviana fussed with the lace on her shoulders as she gazed in the mirror.

"I just got you back, my beautiful child. If I could keep you here forever, I would, but you are meant for such great and dangerous things. I want to protect you, but you have to learn to do that for yourself." Queen Loviana hugged Viviana, who couldn't help but become teary eyed. She felt so much love from the queen and wished she could feel the same for her.

"I'm not ready to face all of this, but I accept the challenges. I've never backed down from a fight, and I won't start now. I will protect my family and all Dragoonus. No one deserves the tyranny of that mad woman."

"That's my girl. You will make a fine queen," she said as she stroked Viviana's cheek. "I will send my best men with you."

"I just need Anthony and Remus…"

"About that… we have changed him." The queen smiled and Viviana's eyes widened.

"You made him human! I knew you would!"

"It was not me, my dear. It was my half-sister, Felisiana. She is the full-blooded sister of Raphiana. In fact, they look very similar."

"Well, let's go meet her and everyone else. I'm starving and I'm sure they are waiting for us." Viviana checked her hair in the mirror and smiled.

"Should I get anything else?" the queen asked.

"No. I have everything I need." She looked at the queen and then gave her a hug. "I know it might take time, but I feel like we could have a great relationship."

"I hope so, Viviana."

"Call me Vi. Everyone close to me does."

"Alright, Vi. Let's go. I'm starving too." Queen Loviana smiled, and they walked together back to the grand dining hall.

213

Chapter 26

When they arrived, the noise of shouting and swords clashing made the two women hurry into the middle of the room. They saw Cornelius and Anthony locked in battle. Viviana screamed for them to stop. They both turned to see her and the queen. The anger on Cornelius' face made the queen nervous.

"You!" Cornelius lunged at the queen. Viviana placed herself in front of the queen. She took out a small blade from her waist and deflected Cornelius' blade. She then punched him in the gut, which sent him to the floor.

"What the hell?" Viviana said as he lay there trying to catch his breath.

"How could you…" he gasped. "How could you let her in here?" He pointed to Lady Felisiana. "She's HER spy!"

"Oh, Cornelius. You never did trust me. I guess you are still upset about that time…"

"SHUT UP," he spat at her as he got to his feet and walked towards the door. The guards surrounded him and

215

tried to confine him. The queen, however, waved them off, and he walked away.

After eating and trying to enjoy themselves, the queen, Viviana, Anthony, and Remus, joined Cornelius and Aurora in a small library to talk.

When they arrived, they found Aurora trying to calm her husband down. The flames in the fire rose and fell as he paced the floor. He didn't look at anyone when they entered the room. Silently, they found seats and waited for the queen to speak, but she just watched Cornelius's behavior.

"Are you done examining me, your majesty?" Cornelius said through his teeth.

"Your aunt…"

"Don't dare call her that. She may share my blood, but she is nothing to me." The flames of the fire burned brighter and filled the room with an intense heat.

"I have her side of the story and I would like yours." She motioned to Remus, who got up and opened a window to let in some cool autumn air.

"That witch had me locked away in a dungeon for a month. She claimed I had burned her on purpose and that I wanted to kill everyone by setting our home on fire. I never would have…" Cornelius stopped as he saw the flames dancing from his fingers.

"You may not have meant to hurt anyone, but I am afraid you did. Your memories are fragmented by the trauma that took place at such a young age." The queen sat waiting for Cornelius to calm himself down.

"I knew you were like me, Cornelius. But then, how does the bloodline work with this power? How is it he and I both be fire starters?" Viviana was confused.

"It's called pyrovoci. You use your own energy to call fire to you or from your own body heat. This is a rare form of didymos. Only a few every hundred years are born with such power at their fingertips. Cornelius, yours was triggered by the traumatic experience from your youth, but you have tried with all you might to block it," the queen said, sounding very impressed with his control.

"The knight's attack triggered mine." Viviana shuddered at the thought of what she did.

"What does that woman claim happened? All I remember is a horse and waking in a cell. I was only seven," Cornelius said calmly, with a note of sadness in his voice.

"She said that a nobleman was beating on a horse and a stable boy, and you stopped him. He grabbed you and you burned him. Your aunt stepped in and saved the man, but at the price of her own safety. You did hurt her, but not on purpose. Fortunately, she has wonderful healing powers and only sustain very light scars on her hands. She told your mother what happened, and she threw you in the dungeon to protect you from the nobleman. He wanted you hung for your crime. Your mother and aunt tried to wipe the man's memory, but he died during the process. So that's the other side of the story," the queen finished, and Cornelius just sat motionless.

"So that's why you make yourself out to be such a pompous royal pain in the ass," Anthony said, breaking the silence. Cornelius laughed.

"You are right. I swore never to give a damn about anything or anyone. It only causes pain," he said, looking up at Aurora, "and then I met you, my love. You helped me out of the darkness." She ran to his chair and hugged him with all her might.

"Enough mush!" Remus said and smiled.

"I apologize for my behavior and accept any punishment you have for me," Cornelius said as she bowed to Queen Loviana.

"Then you and your beautiful wife will have lunch with me and Lady Felisiana tomorrow. We need to get to know our family, and that includes Viviana and Anthony." She smiled at them.

"And it looks like both of you could use the training for traveling to Gaiana's. I will inform the Sun Shrine trainers that they have two students." The queen stood and yawned.

"Tomorrow will be a long day, so everyone please get some rest," Remus said as he offered his arm to the queen, who hooked her arm around it. They chatted quietly as they walked down the hall.

"Remus and the queen? So, he's the knight, and she is that woman he talked about in the woods." Viviana smiled and made Aurora rub her head.

"Of all the things that you have to think about, that's what was on your mind?" Aurora rolled her eyes and Viviana shrugged.

"Well, he's the one she has had feelings for all this time, and they deserve to be happy." Viviana smiled.

"Don't forget their old feelings for each other is the reason you almost got killed as a child." Cornelius pointed out.

"For now, nothing is more important than sleep." Aurora placed her head on Cornelius' shoulder.

"Alright, my love. To bed we go." They started out the door.

"See you two in the morning." Aurora winked, and the pair blushed.

Once they were alone, Anthony gently wrapped his arms around Viviana and kissed her deeply. She melted again. He couldn't help chuckling as he scooped her up and carried her to a chair. They sat together as he ran his fingers through her hair. She brushed her fingers through his well-trimmed beard and planted kiss after kiss on his full lips. They stayed locked in a kiss until neither could breathe. Anthony stopped Viviana as she tried to move her hands lower down his chest.

"What?" She smiled as he kissed her hand.

"If we continue, I will not be able to walk." Anthony grinned as her eyes grew large and she jumped from his lap.

"I guess you should escort me to my room," she said with a note of sadness.

"Good idea. Even though I would make you mine right here, right now, if you let me," he whispered into her ear. He made her shiver and toy with the idea. She knew it wasn't the right time for them.

"I think we should take our time and when we are truly ready, then I, too, would love that." She kissed him and took his hand. They took their time saying goodnight as the rest of the inhabitants of the shrine slept.

Once Anthony left, Viviana let the comfortable bed and cool fall breeze lull her to sleep. She readied herself for whatever came her way. Her life changed so quickly, and she had more coming. She hoped that her strength would be enough to beat Raphiana and her army.

Chapter 27

For the next three months, Cornelius and Viviana studied the old texts to find out more about their heritage while training with Master Tyrainus. They learned how to hone their powers while controlling their emotions. They worked for hours during the day and talked about the training all throughout the evening. Aurora and Anthony aided the pair when they could, but they had to plan the next leg of their journey.

"Stop eyeing them like there is something going on between them. They are training." Aurora drew his attention away from the pair to show him some information about the trip.

"I can't help it. I finally can be with her, and I cannot get a moment of time with her. I'm just a little envious," he said as he studied the paper she handed to him.

"I understand that feeling, believe me. I miss my time with my husband. However, our job in this matter is just as important."

"And that is?"

"Support and love. They need stability to keep them centered when they leave here. They need our love to keep their emotions in check. Queen Loviana gave me this map to help prepare us for the journey. However, after this road," Aurora pointed, "we are on our own. Gaiana possesses this piece of land from there," she pointed to the map, "to the edge of the other side of the forest. She has made it quite impossible for travelers to go anywhere near the Nocaetam Vaille."

"Great," he grumbled. "That makes things a little more complicated, doesn't it?"

"I know, but you are a great knight who has traveled to many uncharted territories, if I remember correctly." She smiled, but realized he was not. "Sorry, forgot that's a touchy subject for you."

"My experience, good or bad, will serve us well in our travels. I'm just nervous and I don't want it to make her nervous. I don't need her to be jumpy."

"Make who jumpy?" Viviana asked, as she tried to catch her breath.

"Are you alright?" Anthony handed her a towel and a pitcher of water.

"Yes, just exhausted. Now, what were you two talking about?" Viviana raised an eyebrow.

"The journey and the lack of information on the terrain." Aurora handed a glass of water to Cornelius.

"Ah, I can see how that could make you nervous. I don't see why that would make me nervous, though. I trust you and whatever we have to face, Anthony. Not only are you my protector," she snuggled up to him and wrapped her arm in his, "you love me. I know what love can do. I'm a prime example." She smiled as he gave her a peck on the cheek and squeezed her hand.

221

"Aww, you two remind me of us," Aurora said as she grabbed Cornelius and wrapped him in a loving embrace. He kissed her with such passion it took her breath away and she blushed.

The four became closer than anyone had expected and created a strong bond they would need. Viviana thought about the danger ahead and wanted to run away with Anthony somewhere they could grow old together. However, she also loved her family and friends. Running away would solve nothing. She had to stand and fight for her kingdom, for her land, for her friends and family.

"Vi," Anthony's voice pulled her back to the group and the planning session. "Are you going to go pack? I think we should all be ready to leave before tomorrow." He smiled, and she shook her head.

"I have to do something first." Viviana left to find the queen. Her chest ached at the thought of traveling again. It seemed to never end, and it made her long for her home. She spent most of her life in a small community filled with the same people, smells, and sounds every day. She wanted to just stop and rest a little longer, to have some time to just be. However, they had to find and secure her great aunt; a woman who had removed herself from society for a reason, a very deadly reason from what they knew.

"Viviana," a familiar husky voice called to her.

"Re... I mean Theron. How are you doing?"

"I am well, little one. And I will always be Remus." He smiled, but it quickly faded. "You looked troubled."

"Just nervous for the next leg of the journey." She twirled a strand of hair around her finger.

"Well, I can understand, but you have Anthony, Cornelius, and Aurora to help you. At least you are not alone."

"It is comforting to have them. I'm just so homesick. I miss the smell of Mathilda's baking bread and the sound of her father's voice as he calls for me." Her voice quivered as she talked. Remus pulled her into his arms and hugged her with all his might.

"I can't breathe," she gasped, and he let go just enough for her to rest comfortably in his embrace.

"I know I'm not your father, but I hope this will help."

"Thank you, my dearest and oldest friend."

"You shouldn't call me old," he kidded with her.

"Well, you are old," Viviana wiggled out of his arms before he could tickle her.

"You ungrateful child," he growled and then laughed.

"Am I interrupting something?" the queen asked, while suppressing a smile.

"No, not at all. Remus was just having a hard time accepting the fact that he is old." Viviana made a high pitch noise when he grabbed at her.

"Alright, you two. I think you both are acting like children," she laughed at them.

"Mother, I was coming to find you." Viviana watched Remus out of the corner of her eye.

"What do you need, my child?" Queen Loviana asked with a big smile on her face.

"Where is the grave of the princess?" Viviana's question made the queen look uncomfortable.

"It is just outside the capital city, Luminox, with the other royal tombs. Why do you ask?"

"I wanted to pay tribute to the one that has guarded my life all these years," she said quietly.

"I see," the queen said with tears in her eyes, and she hugged her daughter. "It is time for dinner. Let us go enjoy our last meal together." They left the library and went to the dining room to meet with Anthony, Cornelius, and Aurora.

The dining room was a small room from the third-floor kitchen. They only used this floor for royalty and their guests. Queen Loviana motioned for everyone to take a seat after she sat down. Each couple sat by each other, with Viviana to the queen's left and the Remus to her right.

"Tonight, we celebrate the next journey for these brave young travelers. You embark on an adventure that will determine the fate of our kingdoms." Queen Loviana raised her glass, and everyone followed. "May you find the path to success and be safe during your travels." She drank deeply from her glass and smiled at Vi.

"Now let us eat." Remus grabbed a turkey leg from the plate and took a bite.

"Don't have to tell me twice," Cornelius said as he took a spoonful of mashed potatoes. The group ate dinner and conversed until late into the night. This was their last night before leaving in the morning, which made Viviana nervous. They were leaving the comforts of the shrine and her newfound mother.

"Vi?" Anthony's voice made her look at him. She realized they had left the dining room and were at her door.

"Oh, my room. Sorry, I was lost in thought, I guess." Viviana played with her hair, trying to get a loose strand back in place.

"I know. You stopped talking right before we finished with dinner. I assume you are worried about the journey?" His question made her shift her weight as she looked at him. He smiled and kissed her head sweetly. "You have me by your side. Plus, Cornelius and Aurora. I can't believe I said that…"

"I know. It's crazy to imagine that they are our friends now. And you are right. I have you and them and myself." She hugged him and felt the warmth of his embrace. "We will make it. I know we will. There are just so many unknowns this time."

"And we will get through it. Get some rest and I will see you tomorrow, my love," he whispered the last two words in her ear. She shivered and pushed him away.

"Goodnight, my knight. Sweet dreams." Viviana pulled him in and kissed him hard on the lips. She winked at him and went into her room. Closing the door, she put on her nightgown and took out her journal. She lit a candle and wrote down the events of the day. Her heart, even with the upcoming journey, felt light and filled with love. Holding on to this feeling, she blew out her light and let the lull of sleep take her away to dreamland.

Chapter 28

The morning of their departure was bittersweet for Viviana. She enjoyed her breakfast with the queen. They talked about everything. She soaked up her mother's smile, her laugh, the way she held her teacup. She wanted to remember every detail about her newfound mother.

"I don't want to leave, but I know I must," Viviana sighed as they walked to the stables.

"I know, my dear child. I feel the same way. However, you have mastered many of the techniques and still are having trouble with control. Anthony was very forgiving when you set him on fire the other day." The queen tried not to chuckle.

"He started it. If he would just leave it alone... I wouldn't be so angry," Viviana whined.

"He loves you," the queen whispered. "He wants what any noble man wants. In this land, and in Dragoonus, we teach our girls that our virtue is sacred. We should save our bodies and minds for the right man. If you have the freedom to marry a man of your choosing, let him be the first man to have you, all of you, since this action has consequences that follow it."

"I have had the same speech from my mo…"

"From your mother. It is fine, Viviana. She was your mother as well as I am. Do you not wish to marry?"

"Can I marry whom I choose? Am I allowed to marry a knight?"

"You are free to follow your heart. In the end, you will be the Queen of Dragoonus and must decide how you will rule. You can change laws and with those changes there will come a new time for the land. I would, however, think long and hard on this matter. There is no time like the present to live life to the fullest, even while facing uncertainty." Viviana could tell that the queen was not just talking of her love for Anthony, but knew it was not her place to speak of such matters.

"Mo…" Viviana stopped once she caught Anthony out of the corner of her eye.

"Are you ready to depart, Vi? The horses are waiting, and daylight is getting shorter now." He smiled as he stared into her eyes.

"Yes, we were just saying our goodbyes." The queen kissed her sweetly on the head and gave Viviana, her only child, a bear hug.

"I will miss you," Viviana said as she hugged back.

"Anthony, please take care of yourself and my little girl. Vi, you take care of Anthony and the rest of the group. Come back to me when you are ready. I will send a message if anything changes in Dragoonus. From what my sources say, we still have time as Raphiana builds her monstrous army and tries to find allies in some of the smaller kingdoms. I have my own ambassadors trying to counter her offers. She has all but depleted the kingdom with her plans."

"Thank you, mother. We will return as soon as I have a chat with Aunt Gaiana. I must convince her to either fight with us or stay out of the battle all together."

"And help us with our powers," Cornelius piped up.

"That too," Viviana added.

"May the road lead you back home," Remus said as he quickly hugged Viviana. They waved until they could no longer see them.

After two days on the road, they stopped in a small town on the outskirts of the capital city. The travelers rested in a comfortable inn. The smell of warm bread and stew made everyone hungry. They sat at a table near the fire and soaked in the time off the road. The ladies were giggling at a charming young boy who came by, asking for a dance as the fiddle player strummed a song. The men watched a young tavern girl try to keep her head on straight as a young lad followed her, begging for her hand in marriage. They all heard some cursing coming from the back as the sound of glass and the shrieking of a cat filled their ears. The vitality of the inn reminded them of their journey and how they would only have each other to rely upon. Aurora looked at her empty bowl and sighed.

"I forgot how hard it is to travel. I will miss the comfort of the Shrine."

"I will miss the soaking tubs," Viviana said and blew a loose strand of hair from her face.

"I'm going to miss the water throwers. I don't know how I'm going to be put out while Vi practices on me." Anthony laughed as Viviana blushed and stuck her tongue out at him. "Is that how a lady would respond? So childish."

"Well, I'm going to miss the food and the bed." Cornelius was picking at the stew. "I wondered what meat this is." Everyone laughed.

"I think it's time for bed for me," Viviana said as she yawned. Anthony pulled out her chair and offered her his arm.

"Goodnight." Aurora smiled as they walked away from the table and up to the rooms.

"Goodnight, Vi," Anthony kissed her sweetly. "I will be next door if you need me." He bowed as she opened her door.

"Goodnight," she said as she closed the door behind her. She could feel her heart racing as she thought about venturing out alone to the gravesite, but she needed to go without Anthony there. He would just get in her way. Viviana went to her bed and settled to read a book and wait for everyone to fall asleep.

Once the moon hung high in the sky, she grabbed her cloak and headed to the barn. She found Moonkiss munching on some hay and offered him a juicy red apple.

"I'm glad you liked your treat, my handsome man. I think you and I should take a quick ride, like we used to do," she said as she climbed up onto his back. He let her guide them through the moonlit night. As she held onto her hood, they rode through the mist gathering around them, illuminated by the moon. While riding her black cloak gave the illusion that a shadow rode on the back of Moonkiss. She kept her eyes on the road until she spotted a metal gate that twisted and turned like snakes dancing over each other. The key for the lock was visible, as if left for her. She heard a footstep, then heard her horse let out a grunt. Then Viviana saw a shadow out of the corner of her eye, and she crawled to a crouching position. She prepared her dagger for the kill, but before she could pounce, Anthony took his hood off and stood far enough away that she could see him but not hurt him, hopefully.

Stunned by his presence, she wasn't sure how to feel about his presence there.

"Anthony," she said through her teeth.

"Sorry, Vi. I shouldn't have taken the key from your bag, but I had to make sure the place was safe before you arrived. Queen's orders." Anthony moved slowly to open the gate for her.

"I love you, but I don't like you right now," she said, giving him a peck on the cheek and slugged his arm.

"Ouch. Fair enough. I guess I deserve that." He took her hand, and they walked through the royal graveyard together.

"The grave is just over there. I will stand guard at the gate." Anthony left her to see what she needed to see, her own grave. She found a beautiful rose-shaped gravestone with her name on it.

"Here lies Princess Auriana Cleopatra Viviana, daughter of King Demosthenes and Queen Loviana. A sweet rose lost before it could bloom." She cried. Through her sobs, she talked to the headstone. "Sweet Viviana, you were forgotten, because you took my place and I yours. You left this earth and gave me a chance at life. You left this world far too young. I will make sure we honor your memory when you are we bury you with your proper birth name. People will know what your family sacrificed for me, and I will remember the stories the queen told me of you. How we used to play together in the fields and chase butterflies. I hope this will please you and your family when they visit." Viviana placed a bouquet of purple roses on the ground as she wiped her tears away and took a deep breath. She walked to the gate and smiled at Anthony.

"My love?" Anthony could see she had been crying.

"Yes. I finally have peace about everything. Even though it wasn't me in there, it felt like it should be. I know she died from a fall and not because of me, however, her death gave me a chance to live. People have mourned her as the princess all these years, but I promise I will make it right when all this mess is over. We both will reclaim our identities." Viviana placed her hood on and watched Anthony bow to her on one knee.

"I pledge my allegiance and life to you, my queen." He rose and placed a small sapphire ring on her right middle finger. "I also pledge my undying love to you and only ask that you consider me as your husband one day."

"I promise to consider it, but for now we have a long journey filled with danger and if anything happened..." She couldn't finish the sentence. He put his arms around her and squeezed lovingly.

"I guess I just have to keep asking until you say yes." He chuckled.

"I like that idea." She snuggled against him. "I love you, Anthony. I will say yes, just not today."

"I love you too, Vi."

"We will get through this, won't we?" She sounded scared.

"Yes, we will." Anthony said with determination. "Let's go back to the inn. We both need our sleep." Anthony yawned, which made Viviana yawn. She leaned against him as he guided her over to her waiting horse.

"I could use some sleep," she said as she mounted Moonkiss.

As they rode, Viviana hoped Anthony would keep asking her to marry him. One day she would say yes and have the perfect wedding. However, until then, she was content with his love and protection on the next leg of their journey to Great Aunt Gaiana and the Nocaetam Vaille.

Once they reached the inn, he escorted her room, and they parted ways. As she settled into her bed, Viviana thought to herself, *soon we will know more about my powers and have a new ally, hopefully.* This was her last thought as she slipped into a dreamless sleep.

Acknowledgments

I would like to express my gratitude to the many people who saw me through this book; to all those who provided support, talked things over, read, wrote, and offered comments. I would like to thank J.K. Edits for their editing services. With their help, I was able to craft my story with much needed constructive criticism.

I would like to thank Amazing Things Press for enabling me to publish this book. Also, I am forever humbled by the wonderful donors who believed in me enough to give to my book fundraising campaign.

Above all I want to thank my husband, Thomas, and the rest of my family, who supported and encouraged me despite all the time it took me away from them.

A Message From the Author

Thank you for taking the time to read my book. I would be honored if you would consider leaving a review for it on *Amazon*.

About the Author

Samantha Fidler-Newby was born in California, but has lived in St. Joseph, MO for much of her life. While still being a city girl at heart, she lives out in the country with her husband Tom. They have a brood of animals that keep them company, including her crazy cats—Asoka, Calista, Luna, Princess Buttercup, Hera, Sabian, and Erza—and one dog—Munchkin. When she is not writing her novels, Samantha loves reading, knitting, ComiCon conventions, and going to renaissance festivals. With her two master degrees, she loves to teach English and Communication collage classes.

If you would like to learn more about Samantha and her writing, please visit her website at
samanthafidlernewby.wordpress.com,
like her Facebook page at
www.facebook.com/thegeekworm,
and follow her on Instagram @thegeekworm.

Check out these books from
Amazing Things Press

Keeper of the Mountain by Nshan Erganian

Rare Blood Sect by Robert L. Justus

Survival In the Kitchen by Sharon Boyle

Stop Beating the Dead Horse by Julie L. Casey

In Daddy's Hands by Julie L. Casey

MariKay's Rainbow by Marilyn Weimer

Seeking the Green Flash by Lanny Daise

Thought Control by Robert L. Justus

Fun Activities to Help Little Ones Talk by Kathy Blair

Bighorn by James Ozenberger

Post Exodus by Robert Christiansen

Rawnie's Mirage by Marilyn Weimer

All American Prizefighter by Rob Calloway

Fall of Grace by Rachel Riley and Sharon Spiegel

Taming the Whirlwind by Lindsey Heidle

John Henry's War by Larry W. Anderson

The Brothers' Murder by Brenda Grant

A Good Life by Sarah Rowan

Desperate Reunion…the Promise by Marylin & Nshan
Erganian

Died Innocent by Don Nothstine

Check out these Poetry books/Collections

from

Amazing Things Press

Evoloving by James Fly

Starlings by Jeff Foster

Nightmares or Memories by Nona j. Moss

Tales From Beneath the Crypt by Megan Marie

Palightte by James Fly

Vintage Mysteries by Megan Marie

Tears and Prayers by Harold W. "Doc" Arnett

Thoughts of Mine by Thomas Kirschner

Inner Reflections by Shivonne Jean Hancock

Scanner Code by David Noe

Blanc Mange by Jeff Foster

Zenphoniquely by James Fly

Kin by David Noe

Voices in My Pen by David Noe

Thoughts of Mine II by Thomas Kirschner

Amazing Things Press

Made in the USA
Middletown, DE
14 May 2022

65764401R00144